Not A Love Story

Not A Love Story

A novel by

Jerome Grapel

ABSOLUTELY AMAZING eBOOKS

ABSOLUTELY AMAZING eBOOKS

Published by Whiz Bang LLC, 926 Truman Avenue, Key West, Florida 33040, USA.

For information contact:
Publisher@AbsolutelyAmazingEbooks.com

ISBN-13: 978-1945772139 (Absolutely Amazing Ebooks)
ISBN-10: 1945772131

To Isidore and Ann, who made this book possible ...

Not A
Love
Story

Part 1

Chapter 1

It's Important

*I*t had turned into a beautiful winter day at the tropical edge of the North American continent. The cold front had blown through the morning before with a whole day of gray, drizzly rain, but by the next day the skies had gloriously cleared leaving a blue dome that sparkled like a waxed car. With the help of a winter sun unburdened by the least bit of cloud to fight through, the temperature had risen to a brisk but comfortable 73 degrees. It was the type of day to get out in.

Sam had decided to take a walk. It led him to the end of the Blanco St. Pier, a recreational structure jutting 300 yards into the Atlantic Ocean. Its leeward position on the southern side of the island made it a comfortable place to be.

For almost an hour, Sam found himself blissfully alone with his inner thoughts −or was it no thoughts at all −as he let the sweet touch of the elements caress his body. This emotional isolation was broken when one of those hand line fishermen who frequent the pier, someone whose cooler full of beer was far more important than the fishing, hooked a 6-inch snapper. His 2 little daughters gathered around as he unhooked it and threw it back to Neptune. "Daddy, daddy, what kind of fish is it?" It was a lovely moment. The world was at peace with itself.

Sam smiled for a moment as he watched things as they

should be. He then turned abruptly and headed back towards land. Way back at the beginning of the pier was the figure of a young woman walking out to sea. Even at more than 200 yards, the leading man in this tale thought he recognized her. As she came closer into range his original suppositions were confirmed –yes, it was Edie, the unanimously deemed lovely Edie. Given the almost absent quality of their social relationship, he found himself amazed at how familiar her stride and bearing was to him.

Sam and Edie had had brief interludes in the past. Very brief. They had exchanged courteous salutations. They had never touched. They were vaguely part of the same contour of the island's social structure. They "knew" each other.

Sam continued to look as the woman drew nearer. If they were going to acknowledge their acquaintance he felt the burden to be on him. Boys stalk girls. He could not help but feel a goose pimply tingle of nerves as he made his move. "Hello Edie."

"Oh, hi." The fact that she had already noticed him 50 yards down the pier did not keep her from acting surprised. The games people play.

Sam had never considered himself a confident player in the sport of amorous pursuit. What success he'd had in this most important sphere of life had always come to him in totally unexpected ways. Dates and disco stalkings had never worked for him. Perhaps it was the relaxed state the natural beauty all around him had put him in, but he suddenly felt his actions were not subject to doubt. For a sublime, brief moment, he lost all his self-consciousness.

"Edie, I have a question –"

"It sounds important."

"Yes, it's important, probably much more important than it should be. You see, I'd like to know if you've ever considered, even for the most fleeting instance, sleeping with me." He could not believe he'd said it! It was as if someone else within him had escaped through his mouth. He tried to act as if nothing extraordinary had happened as she pondered the question.

Our leading lady was even more surprised than he was. She had never been particularly interested in this fellow – what was his name, Sam? Steve? – and yet, there was something in his sincerity – or was it his vulnerability – that did not offend her. He was certainly no James Bond, my God, he looked as if he'd just swallowed an insect.

"Going to bed with you?"

"That's another way to put it – I guess."

Two pelicans diving in tandem splashed into the sparkling sea in search of their next meal. Edie turned her head, the noise of their entry having caught her attention. Sam continued to stare at her, such divine acts of nature not having broken the focus of his concentration.

"Well, that's nice to know," he said. "In other words," he smiled sheepishly, "I am not off your list, there is room for hope."

Edie continued to look at the pelicans as they eagerly gulped down their meal. She squirmed slightly, a miniscule pout barely forming on her lips. By now Sam had returned to his more normal self-conscious timidity. "Earth to Edie."

She turned and looked directly at him. "I don't usually like it when people talk like that to me."

Chapter 2

The Problem

"Well –" Sam shuffled nervously and breathed deeply, "that rather leaves us back at the beginning again, doesn't it?" He continued to gaze into Edie's face, awaiting a response that was not forthcoming. He dropped his sight to the ground, again shifted his weight from one foot to the other and tried to resolve some course of action. His eyes unconsciously began a slow trip up the anatomy of the woman, along the firm curve of her calves, deep into the perceived ivory of her thighs to the place where the treasure lay buried beneath a faded pair of blue jeans. He found himself imagining her hindquarters as he continued the northern journey across the plains of her flat stomach, a journey soon interrupted by the firm heights of the famous twin peaks of macho desire. His sight rested for a moment – perhaps more than a moment – before continuing on to the fine chiseled face framed simply by the boyish cut of her straight blond hair.

"Tell me Edie, what is it you'd like to know?" He asked the question as if he were nudging the intellects of a class full of students.

"I really don't know. I don't have the faintest idea what I want from a man anymore."

"But you are interested?"

Edie shrugged carelessly and turned away. She noticed one of the tall ships heading out the channel with a cargo full of tourists on their nightly sunset cruise. "Interested?"

"You just answered a question with a question."

"Not much help, am I?"

Sam glanced again at Edie's breasts, riding high under a loose fitting green blouse. They seemed to have a personality of their own, with the self-confidence of a great athlete. Modestly changing his sight line, he looked out at the tall ship, barely visible along the horizon. "I don't understand," he said, half speaking to himself, "I seem to know."

"Yes, that's quite obvious."

"Yes, my dear Edie, I know. What seems to be the problem with you? Perhaps if I climbed the Himalayas and descended into Tibet to be blessed by the Dalai Lama, that's right, blessed by the Dalai Lama and given the true meaning of life to be brought specifically back to you in a dainty mahogany box resting lightly upon a purple velvet pillow, transported by me across the shrouded heights of the Himalayan nightmare, delivering such privileged information from the Dalai Lama himself because he felt me worthy enough to present such enlightenment to the woman of my dreams –"

"What is the secret of life?"

"The secret of life is that you Edie want me Sam." He laughed self consciously, unsure as to his course of action. Edie was glad to have had his name confirmed.

"That depends on who is putting the spin on what, no?"

"You don't know, do you?"

"Wish I could be of more help."

Chapter 3

The Flow

Sam sighing heavily. "Quite peculiar, don't you think?"
Edie gazing distantly into the tarheel sky. "Quite."

"Tell me Edie, what is it that so complicates this decision for you? Are my arms too short, voice too high, muscles too stringy, hair too kinky, teeth too crooked? Should I be Tom Cruise or Bon Jovi? Do I walk funny, talk too fast, laugh too loud? Should I cultivate a sincere facial expression? Perhaps you like guys on Harleys with black tee shirts stretched across sumo bellies? Should I drink gallons of beer and shout 'rock n roll'? Cologne, mouthwash, underarm spray? I'll get a waterbed if you'd like. Perhaps if I impetuously grabbed your hand –"

Edie recoiled as if she'd just received an electric shock. Idiot, thought Sam, such bold pursuit had never been the recipe for clods like him. He was not Bon Jovi wetting the twats of thousands of horny fans. He rubbed his hand as if it had been burned by Edie's rejection. Like a misbehaving dog trying to regain his master's favor he barely uttered "still can't decide, eh?"

"No, but you're losing ground."

"Perhaps you'd like to be taken, like a cat in heat –" shut up Sam, what are you doing!

But Edie was not offended by such a remark. She thought how long it had been since she'd actually felt desire, the pure, uninhibited lust for the sight of a slick, hard cock.

"Maybe."

"Maybe?"

"Sorry Sam, I know little at this point."

He loved hearing his name on her lips. "Are we back at the beginning of the run?"

"I'm afraid so."

"Go with the flow?"

"Is there any choice?"

Chapter 4

Getting Nowhere

The annoying buzz of a group of dervish-like jet skiers broke the momentary spell of our searching-for-love couple. It was as if a holy place of natural beauty had been profaned, as if the cathedral had been invaded by barbarians. Now that the island had become a major "tourist destination," much seemed to have been profaned in the last few years.

Edie turned and started to leave. Like water running down a slow drain, Sam could feel his opportunity seeping away. He felt helpless. He had nothing more to say. He'd had his chance with this lovely woman and the game winning field goal had gone way wide. He might never have the chance again.

But the young woman wanted to get the last word. She suddenly wheeled around and spoke almost with anger. "Tell me Sam," he felt as if the Governor had just saved him from the electric chair, "what exactly is this fascination you and your ilk –" she seemed unsure. "Let's put it this way: why is it that your eyes are always riveted to my chest? What is this fascination with gazing at me, what does the roundness of my butt have to do with anything?"

"I think it has to do with procreation."

She ignored what Sam had thought a great line. In truth, she was too immersed in her own intellectual funk to find humor in anything. She continued as if she hadn't heard him. "Beauty is everywhere, don't you agree?"

"Sure."

"Don't you think the trees and flowers are beautiful?"

"Definitely."

"Don't you think the rivers and birds and mangos are beautiful?"

"I love mangos."

"Don't you feel the moon and stars are beautiful, and the sunsets, the gentle rain, the thunder and lightening, the mountains, the prairies –" she tailed off, beginning to feel a bit silly, "and shopping centers?"

"Shopping centers?"

"Oh God," she laughed at herself and her unctuous self-righteousness. "Just testing."

"Did I pass?"

"For the moment." The jet ski adolescence whined monotonously into the beautiful seascape – bzzzz. But Edie had a point to make. "Can you explain why none of these beautiful things give you a hard on?" Why ask, he thought, as he gazed out at the swirling group of jet skiers in their mindless attempts to ward off boredom. Edie continued, "Might you concur in saying, my lustfully longing friend, that we seem to be getting nowhere."

"Concurred."

Chapter 5

Ann Landers

Our story now reaches one of those awkward silences that are so prominent in destroying prospective love affairs. Sam and Edie, standing separately together on a splendid day at the tropical extremity of the North American continent. Is that possible? No matter, suffice it to say they were physically close enough to be together, yet they were both quite alone. They were together in their aloneness. Confusion, ambiguity –nothing.

"To be quite frank, my delectable Edie, there must be more to life than this rutting syndrome we are all helplessly enslaved to –"

Sam was busy digging his own grave in a last ditch effort to save the day, when the divine intervention of Venus rescued one more chance from the jaws of rejection. "Oh my God," exclaimed a genuinely concerned Edie, "you're bleeding!"

Our hero had shaved that morning, slightly nicking himself at the corner of his mouth. Having spent the last few minutes flapping this part of his anatomy, the cut had come open. A thin dribble of blood had started to run down his jaw.

"Where?"

"Right here, look –" She unhitched a small purse that was tied around her waist and took out a pack of Kleenex. Soon she was dabbing the corner of his mouth, gently, almost lovingly. She's touching me, he thought. When she had finished, he felt energized, ready to throw himself into the fray once again.

"Do you realize at one time in my life I was expected to shave everyday."

"Shave?"

"I cut myself shaving this morning."

"Oh."

Sam continued, "Everyday, pressured into it. I incurred favor by having done this shaving task. Each morning I would peer through a dense fog of awakening only to see a grizzled creature which eventually turned out to be me. It was now my unwavering duty to assault my face with that implement of destruction known as a razor. Everyday! Where in the world might such ideas have been promulgated?"

"Gillette?"

"My dear Edie, you have a sense of humor."

"The Gillette God is not so funny."

Sam was beginning to get ga-ga over this woman. What a gem she was. Her sarcastic cynicism felt right in his groove. Gee –

There were now 5 pelicans diving in tandem and there is still the chance our fair damsel might decide to leave. She begins hitching her purse around her waist –

"Edie –"

"Yes?"

"What can be done?"

She laughs. The tension is broken. "Oh my, that is a tough one. What can be done? I think all we can do is hang tough until these evil days of Gillette Gods are over and done with."

"When will that be?"

"Who the hell am I, Ann Landers?" She finishes zippering her purse. "Well Sam, it was nice –"

"Wait, Miss Landers!" He composes himself and tries one more gambit. "Dear Ann Landers, Is it true we shall all be forced to persevere through these pestilential days of Gillette Gods, rudderless as we go, hopelessly outclassed by the times we live in? I can't accept that Ann. There must be something we can do. What can be done? Concerned."

Edie smiles and decides to answer the challenge. She watches the post feeding pelicans sitting contentedly on the surface as she ponders her response. "Dear Concerned, It is best not to concern yourself with questions like 'what can be done?' You would do much better to forget such morbid brain fucks and leave them to the Presidents, PhD's, and Bill O'Reilly. Think more about getting married and mowing the lawn and you will be OK. You can eat Kentucky Fried Chicken, go to Las Vegas and play golf. Stop moping around. This is America, Land of the Free, Home of the Brave."

Back at the shore an elderly couple had arrived with a beautiful golden retriever. Our younger couple watched as the dog slashed gleefully through the shallow water in pursuit of a tennis ball.

"Ann Landers," said Sam, "would never use such language."

"Yes she would. I bet she does all the time."

"Not in her advice columns."

"That's because she's a whore. She's part of the problem."

The dog returned to the slim strip of beach and

deposited the ball in front of its master. The human angst in search of happiness, or fulfillment, or whatever it was that kept humans engaged in their lives, was totally absent in this splendid animal. Sam envied the dog as it lustily shook itself dry and readied for its next sprint into the water.

Sam shrugged and spoke at the pelicans. "Maybe your Ann Landers is right."

"Maybe."

"Seems as if we are back on the first tee again."

"So it seems."

Chapter 6

The Same Boat

$\mathcal{S}$am has an idea. "I say, my ever beguiling Edie, being that I am a hopeful candidate for your affections, and being that I am still on your list, correct?"

"Well –"

"Good enough for me. Why don't we walk along for awhile and further pursue these matters, whatever they might be."

"You know what's being pursued."

"Thank you for such edifying clarification. At any rate, shall we dance?"

They walked back to the beginning of the pier where they turned left and began following a footpath along the edge of the county beach. The winter had been severe and the almond trees on the other side of the road showed only the bright red of the few leaves hanging sadly on its branches at the end of its annual cycle. But this was not a harsh climate and it wouldn't be long before the waxy green leaves of regeneration would begin to appear. The big Poinciana tree, which clung to the wall of the hotel at the other end of the beach, along with the frangipanis next to the beach tennis courts, were just skeletal sticks of wood blown bare by the northern winds. For those not familiar with this environment, they may have even seemed dead. Even the mangrove was browning and thinning out. There was a limbo-like feeling as everything waited for the warmth to return. Waiting. Perhaps this was a good time to feel one's way rather than to act impulsively.

Eventually they reached the other side of the beach where a rickety wooden foot pier ran out into the water. The sun's daily race to the horizon was now in the home stretch as our duo sat down on the edge of the weathered boards and pointed their gaze towards the golden glow. The water just a few feet below their dangling feet, which used to rival any place in the world in clarity, seemed to have lost its edge in the last decade or so, like a beautiful piece of mahogany furniture that hadn't been waxed and dusted for awhile. Was the insatiable global economy claiming another victim?

They sat silently in the glow of the optical illusion of the sinking sun –a minute, five minutes – who was counting? Edie spoke first. "So what do you have to tell me, o lustful one?"

Sam was glad to have her interest, to have her engaged in their mutual company. "Where should I begin?" She shrugged, her eyes closed as she took the orange glow right on her face. "Are you willing to listen for awhile?" She nodded but did not speak. He began his story. "It is difficult to ascertain exactly when things began to go wrong, which really turned out to be right. Those days when things were going right-wrong can only be dimly recalled at this time. It was certainly an era of wealth, though in truth, today's postal employee would be compelled to sneeze snot across my paychecks from those days of respectability, but for the cultural refuse now sitting before this glorious sunset, such white collar income of old compared heftily to the drips and drops which come his way now."

"'Style' was a concept I never seemed to discover in spite of the fact that the paper pushing career I had somehow been culturally directed towards was rather plugged into such double knit pursuits –" He stopped and skewered his face in thought. "What the hell is 'double knit'?"

Edie gazed out at the horizon as the tall ship made its way back to port silhouetted against the descending orange disk. "I'll point it out to you if I see it."

"In any event, I never got the hang of that stuff; style, class, impress a rouged secretary today. My wardrobe always seemed to be in a time warp of sorts, averaging out to perhaps a decade of obsolescence; ties too thin, lapels not wide enough, domestic instead of Italian, get the picture? And the fit! Ichabod Crane looked like GQ compared to me."

"I can see you've finally learned how to dress," cracked Edie, as she scrutinized his white sweatshirt with long sleeves complimented by some faded khaki pants. The sweatshirt had a Florida Marlins emblem emblazoned on the front and a small ketchup stain had found a permanent home on the collar.

"Salvation Army."

"Is there any other place to shop?" They laughed briefly as they watched the tall ship inching its way before the sun. Sam continued.

"I was possessed of an office with bare walls ready to be garnished with the various diplomas I had managed to misplace 'midst the black robed dirges of graduation. I don't suppose the senior partners much liked the sight of those naked walls, but the office was a bit of a cubbyhole anyway and the air conditioner was in deplorable condition, merely, like myself, a stage prop in that theater. Adding to the insult was an ancient Dictaphone lacking the various buttons and switches the more dedicated professionals in the firm grew so adept at using."

Edie lay back and stared into the evening sky. The natural experience was truly magnificent that day. The Earth's dome was so pure in its cleanliness one could almost imagine some mythical window squeegee had just wiped it clean. Venus, the evening star, had just made its appearance high above the horizon. It sparkled in the pristine air.

Sam followed the woman's lead, stretching his back across the warped planks. He went on with his story as he marveled at the celestial splendor.

"In all good conscience, and with devotion to historical accuracy, it must be said I was not worth it. No, not even a foxhole for an office, an antique Dictaphone, and an air conditioner that conditioned no more. No, not even that. I was more of an embarrassment with my wrinkled shirts, diploma-less walls, a desk lacking a wife's picture, perhaps with a young child. My official duties never got much beyond toting the day's documents over to City Hall, though I was given research to do, Bullcrap vs. Horseshit, 27 Pa. Sup. Ct. 375, where it was decided that Rupert Murdoch could become even richer. On the whole, I was not kept too busy. I spent great stacks of time in the lady's john (it had a key) reading anything from Cosmo to Field and Stream. There were rare occasions when I was entrusted to inform a judge that our firm was ready with a case – ready Your Honor – or when I was sent off into the world with a Polaroid camera, my mission being to document the existence of various cracks and lumps in the sidewalk, such municipal negligence resulting in the lumbo-sacral sprain of an innocent, albeit clumsy client."

Edie could not help but cut in. "Boy, I'd rather be here." The sky was now streaked in alternating spokes of blue and orange, a heavenly pattern somewhat reminiscent of the Japanese naval flag, undoubtedly inspired by this not uncommon natural effect.

Sam smiled and renewed his story. "I suppose there was great relief the day I informed my boss I was leaving. I am living proof one does not get fired from such a job, no matter how lame one is, for I was surely nothing but baggage on that train. I was prepared to stay on until a replacement could be found, but as I was suggesting this, my boss, who was busy spraying his hair weave, said no, no, just gather your papers, tidy your desk, shake hands, wishing the best, now I could get a job delivering pizzas. I descended in the elevator, whirled through the revolving door and stepped forth into the grimy urban disaster. I took off my tie and stuffed it into my pocket. From that moment on I left my cultural indoctrination, upbringing, imprinting – call it what you may – behind."

Edie continued peering into the sky. "Were you scared, did you have second thoughts?"

"No. I felt great. It was as if I were a novice ice skater who had been skating awkwardly for hours, ankles caving in, only to take them off and begin walking lightly, easily, painlessly once again. I felt relieved. I had escaped the role my social class had mapped out for me. For better or worse, I had wedded to a life of my own. So far it's been a good marriage with no divorce in sight."

Edie sat up and stared down at the barely visible, yellow

and black striped Sergeant-Major fish swimming just below her toes in the now murky global economy waters. "It's been a perilous journey, hasn't it?"

Sam continued on his back, staring at the sky. "No, not really. It is simply what has led me to you right here on this pier. That puts you Edie, pretty much in the same boat as me."

"Pretty much."

Chapter 7

A Mirage

Venus, the evening star, had begun its descent towards the horizon. It had now become a vague marker in the sky separating the blue violet of the encroaching night above from the flaming orange tones of the dying day below. A smattering of other stars began to appear in the sparkling ceiling of the planet.

"Where were we?" said Sam.

"Somewhere past the beginning."

Sam noticed a lone frigate bird riding the air currents endlessly, without ever flapping its wings. Wouldn't it be great to be a frigate bird? "Oh yeah," now he remembered, "my escape from the world of skyscrapers and doormen in hats reminiscent of Russian Generals was the final escape. Up until that moment, I'd been escaping all my life."

"And you are not escaping now?" asked Edie, almost as a challenge.

The nightly entertainment at the neighboring hotel's Tiki bar dimly swung into gear back on shore – **get back, get back, get back to where** – Sam lip synched the old Beatle's tune as he pondered the question. "Perhaps for people like myself, that's all life is. But that initial escape was the most transcendental, the most difficult." **Get back, get back** – "Here, let me show you what I mean. I say, Edie, would you like to hear an adolescent tale of horror?"

She shrugged carelessly, not showing much

commitment.

"Look, Edie, think of it from my point of view. If you are here listening to my story, you won't be off somewhere else. I can keep an eye on you."

"Sam," shot back an exasperated Edie, "I'm not going anywhere."

"I'm flattered."

"Don't be. This evening is too beautiful to walk away from. Right now, I'd have no trouble sitting here with Jack the Ripper. Go ahead; I've nothing better to do."

"Cool." Sam took a deep breath and laid into it. "Perhaps the most well meaning creature on the face of the Earth is the suburban, middle class parent. This is an animal one must escape from." Edie smiled to herself as if she too could be telling this story. She listened as her companion continued. "One day my father walked up to me and said, well son, it seems as if you are turning out to be dangerously close to downright ugly, a certain donkey-like shape to your jaw, such protrusion being a stain on the good name of this family. How a child of mine, with my Homecoming Queen wife, could belong to such a bumpily contoured mess of a face, flies in the face of all genetic probability, obviously a once in a million mistake easily fixed with a varying array of paraphernalia meant to squeeze and mold you into the beautiful birthright that has somehow, inexplicably, eluded you. We'll have you looking like Cary Grant in no time. Son! We love you. **But dad** – no buts, son – **are you saying I don't look good?** Of course you look good, but it's not exactly what we had in mind. Don't worry, a few years of – **Years?** Yes, a few insignificant years of wired mouths and tooth tightenings, great for blocking punts, ha, ha – **ha, ha my ass, mom and dad, I feel OK** – Not with a face like that. It's all for your own good."

Sam stopped for a moment, insecurely stealing a glance at the object of his performance, trying to measure her interest level. By now, the tune at the Tiki bar had changed – **we had a love, a love, a love you don't find everyday-ay-ay** – "With me Sam, it was just the opposite."

"How do you mean?"

"I was always being told how cute I was, how pretty I was, how lovely I was."

"What's so bad about that?"

"After awhile it becomes your whole identity. You begin to think that's all you'll ever need, everything seems so easy. Life is never that easy. It led me down some very false paths. It was a mirage."

– now its gone, gone, gone, *wo oh oh ooohhh* –

Chapter 8

A Pain in the Ass

Sam wondered if anyone in this world of woe was truly happy. He wondered if such a concept really existed. Maybe we should take it out of the dictionary. Maybe the whole idea of happiness was an illusion that would frustrate us forever. He shrugged. "Anyway," he continued, "mom and dad never seemed to understand." He resumed playing the role. **"You mean I'll have to go to school like that, and have to smile and talk and sleep with it? It hurts mom and dad, I'll be OK without them, honest, I feel just fine, what's the problem? I have friends, I play ball – you have to admit, I hit a ball pretty well. Why are you uptight? Do I embarrass you, does my cousin look better than me? That's it, isn't it! Hey, some people say I look you, mom and dad, did you ever have braces? C'mon, I hate it –** Now, now, you'll thank us later on. It'll all be over in no time. Tomorrow morning, we've made an appointment – **Screw the appointment, mom and dad, such an appointment will make a nervous, neurotic mess of an adolescent out of me, further compounding my burgeoning pimple and zitz problem, my poor posture and gangly, geeky, pubic appearance. In short, I am OK, leave me alone, I am already to the border of the Loco Republic, passport in hand, and one more silly move on your part, mom and dad,**

could get me across the border, a citizen of the Loco Republic. Now, now, son, you must trust us. We are way ahead of you. We already have the name of a good psychiatrist – **A shrink!** – and dermatologists are present if necessary. Your parents know what is best for you son, just a few short years –**Years?** Son, you don't expect us to pull, yank, tighten, twist, heave, crunch, gouge and shape your face, and then deal with the normal insanity – **Normal insanity?** – produced by such, the snippityness of your peers, the inability to eat peanut butter – just a few years of – **Years?** Yes, just a few years, until that glorious day when we shall be proud to exhibit you to friend and relative alike, our son, a son of ours."

The sun had just dropped below the horizon. It was the type of ultra clear day where one might see that illusive, almost mythical concept known as the "green flash." "Sam, I think I saw it. Did you?"

"Saw what?"

"The 'green flash'."

"The 'green flash'?" Sam seemed annoyed, irritated. "You didn't hear a word I said."

A bit further out from where our couple was sitting the old pier disintegrated into a string of wooden pilings popping their heads out of the water. A gathering of gulls pierced the air with their witch-like cackling as they jockeyed for position on the naked outcroppings. "I heard Sam. I heard what I needed to hear." Hardly appeased by her explanation, Sam dropped his sight to the water below, a brooding quality evident on his less than classic face. His thick, dark brows closed in tightly over his eyes. He seemed deflated, disappointed. Edie tapped him on the shoulder.

They looked directly into each other's eyes. She spoke softly, "I heard you Sam, I heard you."

He realized she was still with him, that the game was still on. They smiled at each other. "Did I really miss the 'green flash'?"

"I'm not sure."

"Are you sure of anything yet?" She looked away, gazing out at the horizon. "I guess we are back on Opening Day again, eh?"

"I am a pain in the ass, aren't I?"

From back on shore the dim sounds of music wafted into the air – **I don't believe you, you're not the truth, no one could look as good as yooouu – mercy –**

Chapter 9

Scroogean Logic

For the assembly line tourist that has been persuaded to take their one-week vacation in this place – in much the same way they are persuaded to buy the car they drive or the burger they eat –the sunset experience had now ended. But for connoisseurs like Sam and Edie, the best was yet to come. Although the sun was gone from view, it was creating its most spectacular effects. The lower sky was virtually aflame in a red-orange glow and the Japanese naval flag effect had become deeper, richer, more sharply defined. The spokes of alternating blue-orange color reached behind our duo, almost to the eastern horizon now only barely visible in the gathering dusk.

"Yes Edie, you are a pain in the ass, but it hardly matters in the face of such splendor."

For the next quarter hour they sat silently, immersing themselves in the natural beauty all around them. If the band on shore had been any closer it would have been an intrusion, but, like a rooster crowing in the distance, it was far enough away to enhance the atmosphere. The first set ended to a smattering of applause from the happy hour crowd getting an early start on the alcoholic evening to come.

"Yes Edie," said Sam, feeling the need to re-engage, "you are a pain in the ass, but one cannot be blamed for such behavior as one's behavior."

"Who is?" Sam's timing had been correct. Edie was ready as well.

"There are vast under currents of illogic prodding our minds from clandestine, mysterious places, infesting our perceptions with someone else's idea of who or what we should be. I suppose this is nothing new. All cultures have always indoctrinated its constituents, but in a world such as ours, based almost exclusively on persuading each other to buy a new car, the effect is magnified. For instance, I'm sure you've noticed it is that time of year again." He vaguely indicated towards shore with his head. Although Christmas was more than 3 weeks gone, many houses still had decorations twinkling in the early evening light –the famous "mañana time" of the island. "'Tis the season to be jolly, and I must admit, I don't approve. I seem to be one of those people who root for Scrooge, though I can't say I agree with his financial habits, yet it must be said that most people are pretty touchy with their wealth these days –I mean, hey, nobody's giving it away."

He paused as the squabbling gulls a bit further out on the dilapidated pilings let loose a particularly piercing salvo of aggression. Edie continued to mutely bask in the natural elements all around her. "So now it is the fa-la-la-ing season and we attack briefly during this season of CNN jolliness what is the true reality for all the rest of the year. Scroogean logic is not just the reality, but, sad to say, a necessity in the world of on line trading and cell phone anxiety." He had emphasized the word necessity. "Our whole system is premised upon groveling your life away in pursuit of things you just have enough money for. It's a pretty thin margin Jack, nobody is giving it away."

"Ah hah," said Edie, raising a finger and feigning an intellectual attitude, "you seem to be a classic proponent of

Scroogean economic theory."

Sam lay down on his back once again. The sky was beginning to thicken with stars. "If you must know – I say, must you know?"

She continued to stare at the dimming orange glow. "I'm not sure what I must know. Go ahead, it can't hurt."

"If you maybe must know, the Season to be Jolly is perhaps the crassest perpetration yet to be perpetrated by our crass social code on its fog brained populace. This ignorant mass of targeted markets, during this Season to be Jolly, will be told to buy their children 2 plastic automobiles which, when directed at each other, will collide amidst the clattering of their disintegration; windshields flying, doors coming off, roofs and trunks winging here and there – great fun for junior; simulated automobile crashes. How charming."

Edie chimed in. "Perhaps it is an educational toy preparing him for all those years to come on the clogged highways of his Action News traffic reports?"

"Could be." Sam sat up just in time to see a lone pelican making the day's last dive for food – splash! "But what caught my attention in this commercial message was not the toy itself but its musical backdrop."

"The Little Old Lady From Pasadena?" Edie laughed at her own geniality.

"I say," replied our leading man, laughing as well, "great guess, but – *onnkkk!*" He buzzed it incorrect. "One more try?"

A black cormorant duck, like a natural Stealth bomber, skimmed the water in sonic flight towards the dim glow of the western horizon. Ten seconds later its ever-shrinking

31

form was just a dot fading into nothingness. Our lady furled her brow, shook her head and finally ran out of patience. "I give up."

"As two children gleefully crashed and re-crashed their cars, there it was, dimly entering our sub-conscious, 'stuck a feather in his cap', crash! smash! 'and called it macaroni'. Yankee Doodle, right on, get down!" He took a deep breath and lay down on the weathered boards once again. He seemed distant, far away as he spoke. "I guess automobile accidents are as American as Mickey D's and Hulk Hogan. The death toll on the Season to be Jolly weekend will exceed –"

"Gosh Sam, don't you like to get presents?"

"Not if its part of some kind of programmed mass hysteria."

"But –"

"I've outgrown it. I've come to realize it does more harm than good."

"Oh, c'mon –"

"Christmas is our cultural indoctrination into consumerism."

"But Sam –"

"Affection is much more genuine when shown in other ways."

Venus, the evening star, hovered above the horizon in what little light was left. One could actually see its reflection on the water. "OK, OK, don't expect any presents from me."

"Good. We're starting to understand each other."

Chapter 10

A Crock of Shit

*W*hen the band at the Tiki bar began to play again, our daunting duo knew this night's sunset experience was drawing to an end. Without having to verbally communicate, they got up and headed back towards shore. When they had reached the beginning of the pier they continued walking inland, in no particular direction, with no particular agenda. Sam felt anxiety. Was this the "adios" moment?

"You know Sam," her voice gave him temporary relief, "I think you're cute."

Our man was not overly impressed with such a remark. Many times in his quest for romantic fulfillment, "cute" meant cute, like in let's be friends, I'll try and fix you up with some of my girl friends. When a woman could so easily come out and say something like that, it sometimes meant she felt no pressure, that she enjoyed your company but not for what you really wanted. It could be the kiss of death. But at least the evening would continue – or so it seemed.

"I don't want to be cute," he mumbled almost to himself. Edie recognized the brooding expression she had just seen on the wooden pier when he thought she had not been listening. There was even a bit of anger in play. "I want more than cute."

"OK, OK, you're not cute."

They continued walking down the quiet residential

street. Only the barest hint of colorless light could be seen in the western sky. Night had fallen.

"Sorry," said Sam, "I didn't mean to be rude."

"Oh please, if that's as rude as you get, we can all start calling you St. Sam."

The cathedral was suddenly invaded by barbarians once again in the form of a group of tourists on mopeds. Our couple stood aside as they sped by, bobbing and weaving, horns honking, quickly disappearing around the corner of the next cross street. The sour whine of their motors and the honk of their horns continued to be heard as they belched and farted their way towards the downtown area. A light smell of gasoline hung in the night air. More profanity.

The odyssey continued. It was a somber moment, especially for the male part of the tandem, who could not help but think what a long shot the culmination of his desire for this girl was. He stole a glance at her, walking in silence, not paying attention to him. Without thinking, he let his pessimism get the better of him. "You know Edie, sometimes I feel – like – depressed."

"Oh please Sam, don't start in with *that!*" She seemed annoyed, impatient. "I'm tired of all these depression extravaganzas. People come to my house and confess to being 'depressed'. Somehow, someone like myself, who is not depressed, is supposed to be of help. I find depressed people annoying, probably because they don't seem much different than me. I long for the days when this lush harvest of human neurosis did not exist."

The sudden sound of a catfight, like a needle being dragged cross a record, erupted into their consciousness from some hidden feline battleground. It was over in a matter of seconds. For Sam and Edie, like all veteran island residents, this sound had become a routine part of the environment. Cats were as much a part of your neighborhood as the people next door.

"You're depressed Sam? I'll tell you about depression. There is nothing to be depressed about. Snap out of it boy, none of it is worth it. Whatever it is you envy, want or have lost; whatever it is you desire, yearn, crave or dream about; whatever it is you'd like to be; whatever it is you think is grand and wonderful; everything you lack, all the riches and fame, the glory and conquests, the Lady Di opulence, the home runs and dazzling Super Bowl orgies, all your rock and roll groupie fantasy blow jobs; —none of it is worth it. You will tire of everything —your favorite music, your favorite movie, your favorite flavor, your favorite pair of shoes, even your favorite vagina."

Sam spoke as if he were speaking to himself. "Even that."

"Yes Sam, even that, and you know it." Boy, did he ever.

"Brother Ass." He still seemed to be speaking to himself.

"Brother Ass?" said a perplexed Edie.

"Brother Ass is how St. Francis referred to the human body."

"Why?"

"Because of the gross things it led him to do. I don't think he meant the sexual act itself, but the grossness of the pursuit of sex and what it leads us to do."

Edie seemed a bit surprised. "You don't strike me as a religious person."

"No, no —but you never know where you'll come across

wisdom."

"The problem –" The deafening roar of a Harley on the next block interrupted her. In spite of the intervention of houses and the thick tropical foliage, the sound engulfed them with its uninvited intrusion, so much so that she put her hands over her ears. As the roar began to fade she sighed deeply and began walking. She silently wondered how any society with civilized pretensions could possibly tolerate such a gratuitous invasion of one's privacy. When would these evil days of Gillette Gods be over and done with? Her own words echoed in her mind.

Her anger had unconsciously made her quicken the pace. Sam followed. When he caught up he made her stop.

"You were saying?"

"The problem is that we human beings take ourselves way too seriously. We are all just serving our time here, waiting for the next step into whatever. I've seen enough; what could possibly depress me? Here's my girl friend – she's depressed. She's breaking up with her boy friend of four years, what to do, how will she go on? She's depressed." She paused for a moment, shaking her head, as if to say what foolishness, what a crock of shit. "Her boy friend was a jerk, a certified jerk. What did he have, a golden scrotum? This is what has her depressed? Come, enough of this sludge. All you depressed people, my office is closed. You are all cured – happy, happy."

The breeze was picking up. It carried the sound of a Klee-Klee hawk crooning dreamily in the distance. *Klee, klee.* It was the first one Sam had heard this winter. They usually returned long before now. Why weren't they here? More profanity?

"Ahh," Sam sighed, "if it were only so easy." They walked on. By now the reader might realize that Sam was the more gregarious of the two, the ham, the performer. "You know Edie, up until now you've been rather subdued. What woke you up?"

"Last year I learned a great expression in Spain." She stopped and concentrated as she tried to pronounce correctly in Spanish. "*En una boca cerrada no entran moscas.*"

"Which means?"

"Literally, it means in a closed mouth, flies don't enter. Something like shut up and fish. It's usually a good policy."

"Have flies been getting in my mouth?"

The Klee-Klee bird continued to croon in some invisible treetop. *Klee, klee.* "You know Sam," she was smiling, "I haven't seen a fly since I bumped into you."

For the first time, Sam felt as if he had a chance with this woman. He felt the pressure of it. He could feel the nervous tingle. He might have been blushing.

Chapter 11

Serious Business

*M*oonless night. The transition from day to night had been completed. The people who worked during the day –the tour guides, dive boats, charter fishermen, the moped-jet ski sun in the fun crowd –were either home or at some local's bar washing the day's tedium and tension away with a cold one. The night people –the bartenders, wait people, bar backs, busboys, bouncers and entertainers – were now at their posts, fresh and ready to go. The back streets were private places, quiet and dark. The crickets had begun their nightly chant, the weather a bit chilly for them, but not enough to send them completely into hiding. Every so often, the goose pimply screech of yet another catfight would punctuate the night. No doubt there was a bitch in heat somewhere, the focus of all this macho aggression.

They walked on in silence. Sam wondered if this delectable slice of feminine pie would ever go into heat for him. The natural timidity of his pursuit would not keep him from fighting gallantly for whatever slim hope he could muster. Was there really anything else worth fighting for? Better not to think of such things.

"You know Edie, I've been thinking."

"A habit of yours."

"You're not so bad yourself, what with flies and mouths –"

"Only on rare occasions."

"I'm flattered."

"Don't be." Even in an earlier stage of her post pubic life, Edie was one of those females that always feigned indifference in the face of male pursuit. Having reached a more mature stage of her life, with the usual history of romantic disappointments in the books, she had almost reached a point where she did not have to feign indifference. In fact, such an attitude, if it still fell short of worrying her, was something she had begun to self examine.

They walked by a house with a chain link fence protecting the front yard. In the thickening darkness they had failed to see a rather non-descript black mutt curled menacingly behind it. They passed too close, setting off the canine time bomb ticking away in the early evening gloom. The dog sprung up, barking and snarling in an impressive display of teeth and gums. Although the fence was too high for there to be any danger, the ambush reaped its maximum effect. The woman screamed and they both jumped back reflexively. The dog continued to bark as they gathered themselves. They looked at each other and slowly began laughing. There were tiny pearls of sweat on their foreheads.

From 10 feet away they looked at the dog, who had stopped barking but continued to growl and show his teeth. He seemed satisfied with his work. "Well, ol' buddy," said Sam, wiping his brow, "you got us good, didn't you?"

"I think we made his day," said Edie.

They walked on, staying more to the center of the street. "Where were we?" said our hero.

"Unfortunately, you were thinking."

"Oh yeah. About this depression thing –if there is nothing to tempt you, if nothing is worth it, then what is there to make you happy?"

Our lady was impressed. "Good one Sam. I shall try and explain." She gathered her thoughts and began lecturing, surprised at her own loquacity. "Now children, we have spoken of this thing 'depression' earlier in this adventure. It was then stated there is nothing to be depressed about being that none of it is worth it anyway. Obviously, or perhaps it's not so obvious −"

"It's not so obvious, believe me."

"Patience Sam, this night is made for patience."

"Boy, tell me about it."

"Anyway," continued our fair lady, "this means there doesn't seem to be much in the way of anything to make me happy, whatever that is. Gosh, you might think, isn't that a horrible state to be in? You might even feel sorry for one such as I, possessed with no means to happiness. Such an unlucky girl."

An anonymous rooster with a broken time piece let forth a prodigious call, a useless act which found no response from the more punctual bantam studs in the neighborhood. Our human stud responded; "Look, Edie, I don't feel sorry for you, but you haven't answered the question."

"Patience Sam." They listened as the rooster continued sending unanswered messages. "One thing you can be sure of is that whatever someone might be thinking of me does not depress me. Ah-hah! Some people think I'm a sad person − oh please, only a schmeggegy −"

"A what?"

She laughed. "I have Jewish friends. Only a jerk worries about what others think of them. We are all sad and we are all happy. We all breathe air and crap crap."

The confused rooster tried one more time with equally poor results. Sam could only respect his perseverance. "So?"

"Alright class, quit trying to look up the dress of the girl behind you and listen up – This feeling I've attained of not wanting, of not being tempted, of not needing, of not being turned on, psyched up, or envious of any which thing or person – that *is* happy. Not needing to be happy is happy. Whatever you need was, is, and always will be here; the natural beauty we've enjoyed all day, a planet which provides the means to comfortably sustain us, and, most of all, the wonderful company of each other and all the rest of the flora and fauna. All the things we've been persuaded to desire – the Armani hype, the phone-tablet gizmo with the latest doo-hickey," she paused, consolidating her feelings, "*uuchh*, they are nothing but clutter. They are getting in the way. They are becoming obstacles to happiness –" She suddenly snorted like a horse, shook her head and covered her eyes. "Oh Christ, listen to that shit!"

Sam thought how wonderful it was to live amongst roosters and alley cats, Klee-Klee birds and junkyard dogs, cormorants, pelicans and beautiful women like the one he was looking at now.

"No, Edie, don't be ashamed to say it. Don't ever be ashamed."

They looked into each other's eyes. Something kept them from kissing each other. At this stage in their lives it wasn't a question of shyness – this was serious business.

Chapter 12

The Perfect House

They had now walked back towards the center of the island, the oldest part of town. This is where the city – which occupied the whole island and was known as South Isle – had originally grown out from the seaport area. Like most places that grew up around a geographic advantage – in this case, the commercial possibilities of a deepwater port – the earliest expansions were done in a haphazard way, creating a hodge-podge of streets and alleyways. Ironically, this less than scientific growth now provided much of the picturesque quality which attracted so many tourists. The cemetery, located in the middle of all this, further compounded the confusion, with many streets stopping on one side of it and reappearing on the other. Perhaps the most exotic aspect of this mish-mash of urban irresponsibility was the many lanes – some were dead ends, while others ran through to the next block – that ran off the regular streets. Many of the old Victorian homes were not even located on streets, but were hid away down footpaths, where some of the more affluent recent settlers had created beautiful tropical hideaways for themselves.

Sam had a favorite spot in this area he semi-consciously drifted towards. It was a place where a number of these lanes and footpaths came together in a small clearing surrounded by old wooden homes. The public sector, in a display of intelligent use of taxpayer money, had recently renovated the area, turning it into a "pocket park." There was a small playground for kids; a fancy sliding pond, some swings, monkey bars, and a few benches had been scattered about the area. At this time of day it was usually deserted.

Sam and Edie entered one of the lanes that led to the little park. Thirty seconds later they stood at the edge of the clearing, not quite sure what to do. "Look," said Sam, pointing at a tall stand of Australian Pines on the opposite side of the cozy park, "we can sit on the bench under those trees. They make such beautiful music when the wind blows through them."

Edie seemed tired, even exasperated. "OK, OK, the Australian Pines."

Sam was almost offended. "Look Edie, don't blame me. If you could make up your mind we could get on with it." He immediately regretted such an outburst. He suddenly feared she might have had enough of all this, thanks, nice to meet you, I'm kind of tired –

"I know, I know – you'd think there'd be some way to expedite all this, but we are all slaves to ourselves and there is something about the person that has reached this exact point in my life that keeps me from acting." The wind purred through the trees, *wwsshhh* – "I've always known these trees as Whispering Pines."

"That's the generic term." Thank God, he thought, she's still in the game.

"Makes a lot of sense, doesn't it?" They sat down on a bench under the trees and listened for awhile. *Wwsshhh* – "Ahh, what beautiful music they make."

"That's why they are on the planet," said our boy, as he continued absorbing the sound. A few minutes went by. "If I ever had a chance to build my perfect house, I would have some Australian Pines outside the bedroom window. Can you imagine making love and then falling blissfully asleep to the sweet lullaby of its song?" He was beginning to feel more confident with this woman.

They sat motionless, intensely listening to the tree's symphony. There was poetry here, and where there is poetry there is usually passion and romance. Sam felt excited, sitting there with this extraordinary woman. He felt as if he were flying, as if the sound of the wind were engulfing him, like air passing across an airplane wing. Of all the people on the face of the Earth, he thought, he and Edie were in the best place one could possibly be.

But in spite of the blissful moment, he could not fight back the romantic tension underlying their being together. Should he make his move? Was he missing yet another field goal to win the game? He secretly stole a glance at her. She was oblivious to him, as if the romantic dance that so captivated Sam was not that important to her. Her eyes were closed and she seemed to be breathing in the natural world all around her. He could feel something indefinably special here, something you did not stumble upon everyday. It was useless to try and make the "right" moves. Edie didn't respond to anything like that. He was beginning to realize this was why she so excited him.

"My dear Edie, please don't treat my chatter as an intrusion." She continued to suck in the atmosphere around her. "I have something to say that I'd only –well, I'd only say it to someone who wouldn't take it the wrong way, someone who'd understand. It might seem lewd at first, but it seems to be relevant to what we are currently up to."

She maintained her motionless communion with the elements for a few seconds and then said, without opening her eyes, "Sam," *wwsshh*, "there do not seem to be any flies around here. I'm listening."

Chapter 13

A Shimmering Jell-O Mold

"*I* don't suppose you could ever know how marvelous it is when a post pubescent female yanks a blouse up over her head and off her body."

"I've never given it any thought."

"As it should be, but listen Edie – I've gazed out at Barcelona from the top spires of Gaudi's unfinished church; I've seen the Golden Gate peeking out from beneath the bay fog; I've spied Mt. Olympus glittering in the morning sun; I've been face to face with the enigma of the Mona Lisa – yes Edie, all of that and more, but I can assure you, for a man's man, nothing compares to the sight of a firm pair of female breasts seen dancing free for the first time, oh my, like a fresh shimmering Jell-O mold, liberated from the prudish bondage of a pull over blouse."

"Nipples! Is there a man anywhere who hasn't tried to imagine the crowning glory of the unseen object of his desire? What a global economy assortment of styles, colors, shapes and sizes. Pubic hair. My gosh, it's only hair – but what a location. It's the River Jordan we are all trying to cross in search of the land of milk and honey. Yes, the land of milk and honey, lubrication in its most perfect form, greased and oiled and running to perfection, the most pure absence of self conscious rubbish, the moment we seek 'til the end of our days."

Edie opened her eyes and looked his way, somewhat

flabbergasted by what she was hearing. And yet, something in his attitude, that kind of natural sincerity, or was it that vulnerability she had heard before, kept her from being offended. He was not trying to "make" her. He was just talking, expressing a feeling.

Sam had no idea she had been scrutinizing him as he rambled on. "Warning: this should not be confused with 'love', as it so often is in our culture. This confusion has led to so many problems, that sex and love are beginning to ruin each other, to get in each other's way."

The Australian Pine continued singing its smooth song. Edie spoke haltingly, "You mean, let's define our terms, right?"

"Certainly worth looking into." They sat silently for a minute or 2, thinking back on their own romantic histories.

"Well Sam," she was still a bit confused, "it's not that I regret my previous romantic experiences, but there could have been an awful lot less grief than there was. You see the movies, hear the songs –" she shrugged, not knowing exactly how to go on.

But her companion picked up the ball. "– and you buy into it, right? It takes you so long to realize that an illusion or myth has been created, that sooner or later, you must find love on your own terms, in your own way."

"Yes Sam, but have you found it?"

Sam stared across the little park at the big Victorian house on the other side. He stared but saw nothing. "Have you?"

The dim sound of hens foraging and clucking in some nearby yard caught their attention. Sam suddenly had a change in attitude. "Here Edie, let me show you one of the warped scenes this confusion leads a young man into, let me show you how cynical some of us Monday Night Football Yokels have become."

Chapter 14

A Bit More Style

"There is a universally accepted theory that our species is possessed of only 1 brain, that being located behind the heavily fortified defenses of the human skull. I am beginning to feel like this is a false assumption. Might there not be 2 brains in our bodies?" Edie had closed her eyes once again, sightlessly listening to the pine song, along with Sam's discourse.

"I have this neighbor named Denise. It is Denise and other assorted 20 year olds of her ilk, that lead me to suspect the existence of a brain duality. The brain in my head functions quite admirably when it perceives that creatures like Denise hold no interest for me. This cranial brain astutely assesses her as your typically vapid 20 year old, who, in her case, tends towards extroversion, which is all the more annoying because it means her dormant intellect is constantly being foisted upon me. She smugly considers herself 'cool' for a variety of reasons that include a steady barrage of pounding music accompanied by the off key screechings of what she dubiously defines as music. She takes pride in the fact that she regularly comes home wasted in the wee hours of the morning, as well as the fact that her hymen has long been bludgeoned into oblivion by a numerous array of stiffened male genitalia. Denise is a well adjusted, attractive hormone machine, whose Waterloo of life's disappointments is still a bit further down the road."

The wind had died somewhat, minimizing the chant of the pine trees, leaving a delicious silence in the dark little park, broken only by the crepitations of the insect world which never slept. Edie remained motionless, sightless, a sponge to the stimuli around her. Sam had the stage all to himself.

"Now, though my traditional brain has admirably performed its task in transmitting the fact that Denise is a waste of time, there seems to be another brain in my body which puts forth a different set of data. This brain, vaguely lodged in the region where my legs come together, confuses the issue. This groin brain sends out information confirming that Denise has one of the softest, most pleasantly rounded rumps one's visual field might encounter. This genital brain exhorts me to touch, slide, glide, suck, bite, sit and shoot all over and around this divinity of a rump. This instinct brain is causing me aggravation, locking me in bondage to this fallow-brained 20-year-old. With this genital brain leading me on, I will probably spend a good deal of time with Denise and her implements of musical aggression, pounding my cranial brain into chocolate pudding, all with the hope of sinking into the various orifices placed here and there on her mindless body."

"It's situations like this that cause one to think that the Whatever Deity who runs this universe is no more than a gap-toothed, scraggly bearded jokester, wheezing and cackling sardonically at all the sick jokes He, She or It has perpetrated on us lowly human-amoebas. Sooner or later, with all this in mind, I will no doubt take my burden, carry my cross, put my tail between my legs, and head over to

Denise's apartment, the words 'stop by whenever you'd like' ringing in my ears each time my groin brain pleads for satisfaction."

The litany of insect noises was joined once again by the forage-cluck of the rummaging hens. "Look," said Edie, who had opened her eyes in search of the poultry serenade. The chickens had come out from behind some bushes on the other side of the park. One of the hens trailed a string of chirping chicks behind her. They were oblivious to the byzantine mind fucks of their human neighbors.

For a moment they watched the chickens doing their chicken thing. The soothing sound of the lightly chirping chicks filled the crisp air in the intimate little "pocket park." "But Sam, there's another side to that coin. My side feels the frustration too. How many disappointments have I had to endure when I thought I had it, when I thought this was *the* man?" She suddenly seemed disgusted, giving forth with the horse snort we'd heard before from her. "Jesus! We build such a spiritual cathedral around the sexual act. What colossal middle class rubbish. How many times did *the* man, now that he didn't have to court me, convince me, woo me, how many times did he who seemed so – pardon me Sam – 'cute', turn out to be a perfect bore once the game was won?" They sat silently, watching the poultry troop disappear into the blackened night on the other side of the park. The beautiful chirping could still be heard, like the sound of a far off harpsichord, as the thick foliage gobbled them up. "I don't feel sorry for you Sam, I feel sorry for all of us. I even feel sorry for Denise-of-the-perfect-butt, who will soon find out she'd like to be something more than a perfect butt. I have played out these games a few times too many –"

Sam cut in, "– and we are playing it out once again, aren't we Edie?"

"Quite correct, perhaps with a bit more style, more class, yet still we play, helplessly locked into these tedious machinations so that in the end we can climb aboard each other for a few moments of unbridled whoop-dee-dooery."

"Whoop-dee-doo!"

"I'm sorry my friend, I am still pathetically unable to act."

The word 'friend' seemed somehow regressive or counter-productive to our man. "I suspected as much."

Chapter 15

A Bear Market

They sat for awhile longer, listening to the Whispering Pines, immersed in their own thoughts. It was a dangerous moment, one which flirted with that dreaded occurrence – which was just a convenient way to describe those moments when their being together seemed superfluous, or unnecessary – the awkward silence. Our protagonists, being the mature, sensitive people they were, could feel the tension. They knew this game was far from won and bullshit could never save the day.

Luckily, a big garbage truck, with grinding brakes and wheezing transmission, clattered into the park. The noisy uproar of carelessly handled garbage cans and flying lids and the usual whistles and shouts of the crew getting on with this essential task of human survival, rescued the moment. The smell and racket almost drove them out of the park. They got up and resumed walking.

Their trek took them down a particularly dark street, made so by the dense cover of Malay palms which bordered it on both sides. The trees were healthy, mature specimens, laden with the yellow-orange coconuts that are their trademark. They arched high over the street, intercepting the beige light of the street lamps above. In spite of it being a public way, it was a private place.

Sam and Edie dimly became aware of another couple approaching from the other direction. They, unlike the focal pair of this story, were holding hands. The 2 couples passed without so much as a nod of acknowledgement, in private worlds, at least superficially. They had noticed each other but their own affairs had engulfed the moment and each respective blip was soon gone from the radar screen – but not forgotten.

Sam spoke. "Holding hands."

"Do you think they've done it?"

"Holding hands usually signifies such."

"Usually."

Their journey continued. The dense Malay cover gave way to a clear sky dotted with stars. They were now bordering the cemetery. "Perhaps," interjected Sam pensively, "he took her hand as a rather bold gesture meant to soften her up?"

"Perhaps." Edie remembered Sam's clumsy attempt to grab her hand on the Blanco Street Pier. "I can dimly remember such bold advances. Extricating my hand was always a delicate maneuver."

"Quite so Edie, but at times a hand is proffered by the female as a signal to proceed."

"True, true – I've sent forth such signals in my day – though timidly, maybe just a brushing of the backs of our hands – many of which failed to pierce the thick skull of the gorilla I was wooing."

"'Blowing it' is what we gorillas call it." And God, thought Sam, was he ever adept at blowing it.

Walking, walking. A stout dog with stubby legs hurriedly passed them going in the same direction. He had short hair and was built like a basement boiler. His big ears stood straight up and the click of his paws on the dark pavement resonated in the night. The collar around his neck indicated he was not a stray and he was obviously out of his neighborhood, uneasily heading home through enemy territory. He quickly stole a glance at our duo as he passed, but there was no time to lose. He nervously looked about as the dogs of the neighborhood let him know he was not welcome. Sam wondered if he had gotten the bitch he was after or if his foray had been in vane.

"Interesting," he said, "how things don't work out."

"What things?"

"Oh, you know – do you think our little Cuban cigar dog scored tonight?"

"Oh, that thing."

They turned onto another street which bordered the cemetery in a different direction. The gravestones sat eerily in the dark night, commemorating the fallen offspring of successive generations of whoop-dee-dooery going all the way back to South Isle's beginnings.

"No, Edie, seriously – our romantic endeavors, culturally speaking that is –"

"You mean all of us, not just us?"

"Right. I mean as a culture. Our romantic dealings seem to be going through hard times. There seems to be confusion, uncertainty –"

"You mean things are fucked up."

"Edie, I didn't know you were a poet."

She ignored his remark as they continued on. A purple splotch of thick bougainvillea glowed in the light of a street lamp, like a purple rug climbing the mahogany tree which hosted it.

"You know Edie, I have a friend who watches a

55

particular daytime drama. Soap Opera. She informed me that one of the male stars on this manic-depressive, manic-oppressive show was recently seen in South Isle; restaurant opening, very chic, pishy-poshy restaurant Francaise, and our soapy star was in attendance adding a touch of glamour to the whole scene. Homosexual scene. Men so meticulously dressed and groomed they seemed to be made of shellac."

"How do you know? Were you there?"

"I'm imagining it."

"Then you should be a writer."

The remark caught Sam off guard, took him momentarily out of focus –"Anyway, I'm not out to offend anyone. Everyone is so touchy these days. Really, I have the same gripes with homos as I have with heteros. I consider both groups equally ridiculous. I don't consider my sexual proclivities any more or less ridiculous than theirs. I might consider their sub-cultural style ridiculous, but then again, have you seen all those heteros with rings in their noses or wearing their favorite football player's jersey? I am not annoyed, nor do I look askance at the people who provide orgasms for homosexuals."

"Sam, you're a real humanitarian."

"I am more into the irony of this soap opera thing. Do you realize there are millions of sexually starved women all across the length and breadth of the world's only stupid power fantasizing about sleeping with homosexual men who are their dream lovers on TV? They are so handsome, so charming, so unlike their pot bellied, beer guzzling, armchair quarterback husbands. They are fags. They couldn't care less about Penelope Cruz, let alone that dreamer in hair curlers dragging some snotty kids behind her in the super market. There is irony here, don't you think?"

"Perhaps you paint with too broad a brush —but yeah, I'll buy it."

They passed a house with a big aqua-yellow macaw sitting on a perch in a cage. He squawked out a greeting: "Let's get it on, let's get it on, *aarrraaawkkk!*" The bird caught them by surprise. They stopped and waited for the beautiful parrot to say something again, but it seemed to be teasing them with its silence. Edie continued, "but not everything is screwed up. The Stock Market is booming." The macaw looked out at them, his head slightly tilted to one side, as if it were listening to the conversation. "But emotionally, I'd say it's a Bear Market."

"Makes it a scary thing to invest in, doesn't it?"

"I guess that's why I'm such a pain in the ass."

"*Aarrraawwkkkk!*" squawked the big bird. "Let's get it on, let's get it on —"

Chapter 16

A Slap in the Face

One of the more defining aspects of South Isle's personality is its geographic location, situated directly over the fault line where the Anglo world to the north and the Latin world to the south come together. This encounter of the 2 great cultures –cultures that have been historically antagonistic –has shaped much of what has happened here in the almost 2 centuries since Europeans have permanently inhabited the island. Even the name of the place is a somewhat mistaken result of this culture clash: when the Spaniards, who never erected a settlement here, first discovered the low lying, mangrove island, they found a lot of salt on the beach, perhaps deposited by a recent storm or hurricane. As a result, they named the island "Playasal," pronounced ply-ya-sahl in their language, meaning "salt beach." When the Americans bought the island from the Spaniards, to their ear ply-ya-sahl sounded like island south. Hence, the eventual Anglicized name of South Isle.

Another linguistic result of the mixing of the two cultures is the word used to identify a native of South Isle. The Spanish word for someone who lives on an island is "isleno," pronounced ees-layn-yo, meaning "islander." As the years went by, the natives began referring to themselves as "Lenos," pronounced layn-yos, a word still in use today.

Our pair stood on a corner with an open lot. For as long

as Sam could remember, more than 30 years, the lot had been empty. For such a valuable piece of real estate to remain undeveloped at this stage of the game was something bordering on miraculous. It was probably owned by some elderly Leno – maybe he did not even live on the island anymore – who just didn't give a damn about money or investments or mutual funds or AIG or on line trading, maybe some crotchety old craw fisherman with a bottle of Jack Daniels by his side right now. Undoubtedly, his heirs were eagerly awaiting his death.

Being that the lot was not being cared for, a lush green vine with big oily leaves, in a Darwinian display of power, had taken over the property. There were beautiful white flowers growing all over the vine. Edie noticed them and bent down to take a better look in the dim light.

"Look Sam, the whole lot is covered in these – what are these things?"

He examined the overgrown lot for a moment. "I think they are called 'night glories'"

"It must be beautiful to see them in better light. I wonder why I've never noticed this corner before."

"Because the flowers only come out at night."

"Oh, I see – *night* glories."

On a night requiring great amounts of patience, Sam was not always up to the task. He now felt a bit exasperated, as if he were wasting his time or making a fool of himself. "Yes Edie, night glories." He breathed deeply and gazed into the sky. "Look, maybe we'd do better if we talked about where we came from, or what our jobs are, or where we went to school – you know, stuff that other people talk about."

Edie felt like a balloon the air had gone out of. For the first time since she stumbled upon this – what? – brooding? paradoxical? unpredictable? man, she felt a pang of disappointment. Did this disappointment mean she had developed some expectations from this encounter? She continued looking at the sea of green dotted with the specks of white flowers. She felt let down. "You know Sam, that's the first fly that's gotten in your mouth all day."

He felt the remark like a whip-like slap in the face. He may have even winced. Edie continued staring at the flowers, though she was not seeing them. The crisp winter air seemed to have taken on a heavier state of being. He realized he had erred pathetically. This was no ordinary woman. This was no time for ordinary things. That's why he wanted her so. Remember that, he thought.

"Thanks Edie, I needed that."

She turned around and looked at him. She almost imperceptibly began to nod affirmatively to herself. "Alright, I think you get it. C'mon, let's keep walking."

Chapter 17

What's My Line?

*O*rder had been restored. This story can continue.

"You know Edie, all hyperbola aside, we already have talked about my job – or at least what was once looked upon as my 'career'. What about you? I know nothing. Things like that interest me."

She shrugged and sighed audibly. At this point in their relationship – if it could be called that – she found such a question irrelevant. She didn't have the energy to get into it. "Oh – it's not much different from what happened to you." She was tired of explaining her life to others. "I escaped as well. Let's leave it at that."

OK, he thought, if that's the way you want it – no more flies. The crickets unconsciously filled the air with their background chorus as our couple's particular odyssey moved into whatever was the present at that time. But the loquacious quality of Sam's personality eventually overtook the moment. "In any event, when I was a kid, one of our family rituals was to watch a famous game show – I can't remember the name, but it had to do with guessing what someone did for a living. The panel would ask questions and –"

"What's My Line?" said Edie.

"That's it!"

"My parents used to watch the reruns."

"Wow, you really did escape the same thing I did."

"So what's with What's My Line?"

"When I became a young adult and started thinking for myself, I began to realize that my cultural indoctrination, like all indoctrinations of one sort or another, had not been altogether honest with me. Not being one to mindlessly accept things –"

"Ah-hah," cut in Edie, "you're not going to take Ann Landers' advice?"

Sam threw his head back and laughed, remembering the beginnings of what now seemed to be a great journey. Wow, the Blanco Street Pier – it seemed days ago.

"How about Dr. Phil?" The clown in Edie existed too. He loved it.

Sam continued to giggle. "No, maybe Casey Stengel, but none of those TV clowns. In any event, I began to question everything."

"Ditto."

"I began to write parodies of –"

"Are you a writer?" She wanted to know.

Their ad hoc itinerary was rudely interrupted by the barbarians as the noise and bluster of another pack of moped revelers whizzed by in the darkened night, leaving its predictable wake of honking horns, whining motors and petroleum residues. They looked at each other, wearily shrugged, and walked on.

"Let's just say," he renewed the conversation, "that I write." Unlike Edie, who seemed bored explaining herself, Sam was proud of his literary pretensions, even if he was insecure with its quality.

"Have you tried to get your stuff published?"

"Oh God – I guess I'm always trying – and not trying at the same time. Trying to be a 'success' can be a very degrading activity." As the dimming insinuations of the moped herd faded away in the distance, he wondered if his lack of effort was more premised upon his lack of confidence than on his lack of ambition.

"You wouldn't believe," said Edie, "some of the talented musicians in this town who don't even bother."

"I'm sure we know some of the same ones."

They passed a house with a skinny cactus rising by its side. Like a mythical beanstalk, its spindly form grew 30 feet into the night. Edie thought of the big, pin wheeling flowers it put out in the summer time. "Now those I'm sure of; night blooming cirrus, only at night."

"Right," said Sam, glancing at the Yao Ming-like plant. "Where were we?"

They couldn't remember. They walked another 100 yards before Edie thought of it. "What's My Line?"

"Oh yeah. One of the first things I ever tried to write was a parody of that show. To me, it was magnificent. I would read it over and over again, savoring what I thought to be a great piece of satire. I can still remember it, word for word." He paused, measuring her interest level.

"I suppose there's no stopping you now."

The ham in Sam urged him on. He gathered himself and began his performance. "No, no, panel, we are running out of time. Let me flip the remainder of the cards —wait! Arlene, you think you might know? – Yes dear, quickly –a Ponzi scheme creator?" Edie laughed as they walked on. ""No, I'm sorry. Panel, we shall now hear from our contestant as he tells us what his line is – **Bicycle thief** – Yes panel, a bicycle thief. Clap, clap, clap, whistles, smiles, I don't believe it, shaking of heads, of course, a bicycle thief.

Tell me sir, how long have you been a bicycle thief? **Since I was 8**. Ah, so it's been a long and fruitful career. I say, do you ever feel a bit sorry, slight tinges of guilt, pangs of conscience, that sort of thing? **Nah**. Well, when you think of it, this is a free enterprise system, I guess it's all figured in, some gets bought, some gets stolen, some gets insured, hey, the whole system would fritz out if nothing ever got stolen. **Yeah, 'ats right, ah'm helpin' da economy**. And a noble businessman you are, taking risks and such, just like Exxon. **'at don't seem too risky t'me**. How did you get into the theft business? **Ah'd'know, I just fell inta it I guess. My olda brudda was priddy good ad'it. How did you geddinta 'dis**? Good question. How does one get into selling poo-poo cushions or plastic vomit? Or how about one of those slimy rubber frogs?" Edie was laughing lustily. She put her hands to her cheeks as if they hurt from laughing. Sam hardly noticed as he concentrated on his performance. "Well sir, I congratulate you on your success in your chosen field of endeavor, and wish you a profitable future. **Right on, an' don't faget ta not lock ya' bike, a'right**? – Ha, ha, ha, clap, clap, clap, until next week, this show was brought to you by –"

Sam could see his act had brought the house down. Such moments built his confidence, made him feel more at ease, giving him the opportunity to be more himself as the night wore on. Edie was still laughing. Her mirth became contagious and he began to laugh as well. When she had calmed down she looked at Sam and asked, "Would you like to know what my line is?"

"I thought you didn't want to talk about stuff like that."

She ignored him. "My line is to earn a little cash so as

to have enough grub, some walls and a roof to surround myself with, and a minimum of clothes with which to repel the elements and protect my nudity."

Sam gazed at her. "Your nudity?"

"Sorry I brought it up. All I mean to say is that I am riding out these flea ridden, mangy days of Gillette Gods as best I can until the time comes when we begin living as sane creatures on this planet once again."

"You may have a long wait."

"There is little to do but wait."

"One may try to escape, no?"

"Isn't that what we are all trying to do?"

"What is it, waiting or escaping?"

"Who the hell are you, Perry Mason?"

They laughed heartily as they proceeded into the night. Another inning had been completed; the game went on.

Chapter 18

A Waste of Talent

One of the more poetic results of South Isle's Anglo-Latino cultural fusion is the way in which the 2 distinct parts of the island are designated: the old part of the city, with its Victorian homes and mish-mash of lanes and alleyways, is known as the "Old Barrio," while the new part of town, built with landfill in the last 75 years or so, is known as the "New Barrio."

Although the Old Barrio only took up 1/3 of the island, it was the soul of the island-city, its identity, the place that gave it its unique quality. The Old Barrio was more a way of life than a geographic location, and without it this place would hardly be any place at all.

There is only one recreational park in the Old Barrio, located at the edge of it, just before the main street in and out of town widened into a generic, 4 lane thoroughfare that could be Anywhere, U.S.A. – the car dealerships, the fast food joints, the blinding glow of convenience store-gas stations, the drive thru wasteland that had somehow become accepted as a part of the "American Dream." For people who'd lived the Old Barrio lifestyle with some longevity, going beyond the park was referred to as "going back to the States." It was a hostile world of plastic and neon that one ventured into for only the most essential tasks; going to the doctor, buying underwear, getting a new TV, etc.

The park itself contained a well-groomed softball field, 5 tennis courts, and a basketball court, all amply lit for the usually abundant night action. There was also a green area sprinkled liberally with the dense cover of the old Ficus trees which provided refreshing shade for the picnic tables found under them. Unfortunately, these tables were generally found liberated by that shadowy presence percolating on the fringes of our culture, the "homeless people." A playground for little kids, usually well attended by moms and dads lovingly watching the objects of their affections, and a recently renovated clubhouse with clean rest rooms, a snack bar, and indoor recreational activities, rounded out the picture. Homeless people notwithstanding, it was a nice park our public dollars were well rewarded for.

The well-lit park was like a beacon in the night and our wandering couple could not help but head towards its glow. They entered the park just where the basketball court glowed in the sour light of its evening activity. The usually ragged full court game was raging up and down as our pair strode by.

"Hey ref! You' blind, man."

The remark, to Edie's surprise, was directed at Sam. A young black man with a shaved head and very light skin – what the brothers and sisters call "yella" – was laughing good naturedly as he greeted our leading man. He was a good sized kid, maybe 6'4," with the well chiseled muscle of a tight end. He hadn't bothered to run down to the other side of the court after having dribbled the ball off his toe.

Sam looked in the direction of the voice. "How ya' doin' Bird? I can see you still suck." Bird just smiled and returned to the game when it came back to his side of the court.

Jerome Grapel

Edie looked at Sam inquisitively. "Do you play much basketball?"

He explained how he used to play a lot of basketball but when the knees had started to give out, he took up tennis. That was more than 25 years ago and he had learned to play tennis on the courts in this park.

"Then how do you know −?"

"The Bird?"

Edie looked at the sloppy game in the unflattering light. The player who had joked with Sam had a face reminiscent of a hawk or eagle, mainly in his close knit eyes. "Yeah, the Bird."

When his skills as a player began to erode, Sam had decided to stay in it by becoming a referee. Being that South Isle was about 150 miles from any other high school of its size, he'd been refereeing only the local school's games for close to 20 years. The succeeding generations of local players got to know him quite well. As players they viewed him as their natural enemy, but once they had graduated and left the scene of their high school deeds behind, they generally showed a subliminal respect for Sam's work by saying hello and letting him know they remembered him. In other words, no hard feelings.

When Sam had finished explaining this to Edie, they stood and watched for awhile. "The Bird −his name is Eric Randall − graduated about 5 years ago. He was the best player of his generation. He could go to the hoop like a runaway freight train, strong, physical, but he could also shoot the long one."

The game itself, like almost all schoolyard games, was out of control and undisciplined, but the individual talent

71

of some of the players was obvious. The basketball scene in the park was a fairly accurate cross section of South Isle's population. Being that the white Lenos had forsaken the Old Barrio for the more modern neighborhoods they'd built on the other 2/3 of the island, the white guys were usually young men who'd come here to work the tourist scene from other places. Some of them ended up staying on, but most played out the scene within a few years and got back to something more respectable as they grew into older men. The black guys were usually Lenos, their Old Barrio neighborhood having remained intact into modern times, though some were navy guys serving their time at South Isle's military installations. Their was also a healthy Latino presence, some of them first generation arrivals riding the ever swelling wave of northerly immigration, while others were Lenos or sons of immigrants more comfortable with English than Spanish. About the only thing missing was the gay community, although their presence was felt at the nearby tennis courts.

"You see that guy with the ball now?" Sam pointed to a dark skinned player with short dreadlocks popping out the top of his head like pieces of rigatoni. He was about 6'0" tall and whippet slender, with the stealth and speed of a black panther. "His name is Thaddeus Buford. He was the school's best player last year." They watched him weave the length of the court, leaving everyone in his wake, eventually finishing with a nice reverse layup. "This kid has it all. He got a scholarship to a big time university upstate. When I saw him back in town a few weeks ago, I asked his high school coach what happened. Once he found out he wouldn't start, he packed up and came home." Sam shook his head in a sad expression of hopeless resignation. "Many of these kids can't adjust to leaving the island. The more level headed ones end up digging ditches for the Aqueduct Authority or Streets Department. The more rebellious ones – well, I've already seen Thaddeus in places he shouldn't be. I've seen a lot of talent wasted in this town"

"And the Bird?"

Sam smiled. "The Bird is one of the good ones. He's already started his own hauling business, has a truck, a wife, a kid – he's got good Kharma."

They watched a few minutes longer, until Edie began to lose interest. "Well Sam, the waste of talent doesn't surprise me. Our culture wastes lots of talent."

"How do you mean?"

"When you consider that most of our talented people are doing little more than working for the sale of superfluous things we really don't need, and mucking the Earth up in the process, I would call that a waste of talent." Our lady seemed impatient, edgy. "Sam, I have to pee."

He pointed her in the direction of the renovated clubhouse. "I'll wait for you on that bench in the playground."

Chapter 19

A Long Time

The bathroom was clean and well lit. Opposite the stall where Edie had just relieved herself, was a large mirror hung over a well-crubbed sink. She found herself face to face with her own image as she exited the bathroom stall, an image any human being with the least bit of vanity would find difficult not to be narcissistic about.

She unzipped her small waist purse and took out a pack of Kleenex and a hairbrush. After dabbing some water on her clean-featured face, she wiped it clean with a double sheet of the delicate paper. She then began to brush her short, straight blond hair. Her whole look was consciously low maintenance – no make up, lipstick, no fancy hair do, etc. – and she was done refreshing herself in less than a minute. The clear image in the mirror called her attention.

Edie was well preserved in her mid 30's. From an early age, she realized her good looks were not in doubt. They were the classic example of the American beauty, perhaps best embodied on the contemporary pop scene by a Meg Ryan or any number of blond stars. Her physical attributes had certainly enhanced her stay on this planet, but, as we've already alluded to in this story, she was much more than a pretty face and healthy body. For a sensitive female maturing into a whole person, such a combination, she had begun to find out, could even become a bother. She had broken up with her last serious lover more than a year ago and had begun to wonder if there was any man anywhere worth getting excited about. After a few unsatisfactory sexual encounters, she had even begun to doubt her sexual necessities. What had happened to her youthful passion, when she could even enjoy the sexual act in casual escapades? It had been 6 months since she'd last slept with anyone. Her good looks had become irrelevant. She almost wished she did not have them.

She zipped up her purse and exited the bathroom. About 20 yards away she saw Sam sitting with his back to her on a bench in the playground area. She studied him closely. He had what seemed to be a piece of notebook paper in his hand and he was carefully reading something in the dim beige light above the bench. By now it was almost nine o'clock and the kiddy playground was deserted.

It had been a long time since she had devoted this amount of time to a man. As she watched him from afar, she had to admit his parents were not all that wrong with regard to his looks. He was short, only an inch or so taller than her, but his body was not the problem. He was well proportioned and in good shape, with the sinewy strength of an Olympic sprinter. But his face was hard to reconcile. His nose was hawkish and too big, his chin unfinished and too small, and his low forehead, which was the antithesis of the forever praised noble or high forehead, sloped back at a severe angle under a Brillo-like mop of dark brown hair. If she hadn't already discovered his good-natured gentleness and sensitivity, she might have thought of him as a predatory, medieval moneychanger.

But he had one feature worth mentioning.

As the history of the written word has unfolded, it is

quite possible that the impact of a person's eyes has been over valued by those who indulge in this art form. But in Sam's case, they could not be overlooked. His dark eyes mitigated much of the negativity that might be associated with the rest of his physical appearance. They were piercing beacons of intelligence that interrogated everything they saw from their too deeply set lair. They held the keys to every emotion the human animal possessed. They turned an otherwise unappealing irrelevance into a provocative magnetic force. Sam's attraction was not physical; it was an idea, something that had to grow and take root.

As she approached him on that cool winter night, she wondered if she still wanted the same things from a man that she had sought in the past.

Quit mind fucking, she thought, go with the flow.

Was there any other choice?

Chapter 20

Just One of Them

She stole up from behind in an attempt to surprise him. When she was about to "boo" him, Sam said, without looking up from his notebook paper, "Feel better?"

"Boy, you're no fun." She sat down beside him. "What do you have, eyes in the back of your ears?"

"The back of my ears are a State secret. If you look back there I'll have to have you eliminated."

"C'mon Sam," she said, batting her eyes in mock flirtation, "you wouldn't do that to little ol' me, would you?"

"Well, in your case, I'm sure I could be bribed."

"With what?" The little flirtation game was over.

"I think we've already established that."

She squirmed a bit on the bench and looked away. "I don't think that kind of thing would work for you."

"What thing?"

"Bribery induced sex."

He leaned back and took a deep breath. She was right. She knew where he came from, who he was. He returned to a normal sitting position and turned to look at her. **I don't believe you, you're not the truth** – the old Roy Orbison song wandered into his brain.

She smiled sadly, got up, and walked over to one of the swings hanging limply in the now almost windless night air. She sat down but did not do any swinging. "What are you reading?"

Sam joined her on the neighboring swing. He rocked gently for a few moments before braking with his feet and turning towards her. "Something I wrote in the last few days. I had intended to look it over on the Blanco Street Pier this afternoon, but the beautiful day made me forget it. Then you came along. I forgot I even had it with me."

"What made you remember?"

Sam turned his head and gesticulated towards the basketball court where the ragged game still raged up and down. "It has something to do with that. When you mentioned the lack of sanity on this planet, it made me remember."

"What's that got to do with the sanity on this planet?"

"Everything. I officiated the game at the high school this weekend. One of the traditional powers from the big city was down here. It was a wonderful game between 2 talented teams, and the big city hotshots got beat by the local yokels. The city slickers never seem to accept this fact gracefully. Their coach was very rude after the game and it left a bad taste in my mouth. When I got home, I felt a bit down – like why should I have to take such crap?" He pulled the piece of paper out of his pocket. By now the fold creases were firmly etched into the paper's surface, and the ragged side where the sheet had been yanked from the spiral notebook hung like glitterless tinsel. "In my frustration, I sat down and wrote this."

"What is it – like a chronicle of the game –?"

"No, no, hopefully something more creative. One of the duties of a referee is to bring the opposing captains together before the game, shake hands, how do you do, let's have a good game, yadda-yadda, har-dee-har-har. When I got home that night I decided to write what I would really like to say."

"Can I see it?"

From what we've already learned of Sam in this story, one would think he'd be eager to accommodate our heroine. But he'd learned all too often that giving your stuff out, just like that, really didn't accomplish much. Most people were just being nice —yeah, I'd love to see it —but most of them either never read it or couldn't convey anything worthwhile. They just didn't understand this was something serious for you, that nobody ever "wrote" without real pretensions. Sam had decided, perhaps with a dose of sour grapes —in fact, he knew he was being somewhat insincere with himself —that being a "writer" had more to do with being consecrated as such than with having talent. Once this consecration took place, however that happened, then people began to take you seriously. If not, you were just one of them, no matter how well you wrote.

"Really Sam, I'd love to read it."

"It's the only copy I have."

"I'll read it right now."

"Do you think that's a good idea?"

"Sam, shut up and give me the paper."

Chapter 21

Lolita Cheerleaders

Sam handed Edie the piece of paper. She took it and went back to the bench with the light over it, while he stayed on the swings and began swinging vigorously. She sat down and began to read this:

Alright captains, here we are again, trying to add something worthwhile to the mediocre lives we live, that being a clean, hard fought, sporting game of basketball. First off, let's put on the record that I am not cheating for or favoring anyone, so don't hold it against me, though some degree of disagreement is permissible let's try to remain in the realm of what might be loosely defined as civilized. In fact, it would be splendid if you could all refrain from calling each other niggers and spics and lay off beating on dumb honkies. What's more, it would be positively considered if 2 or more participants from differing teams, red and white in this instance, find themselves wrapped around the ball at the same time, they will heed the call of my whistle and disengage immediately without inflicting too many bumps, lumps, bruises or contusions to your opponent's body. In addition, and although I know this next request is fully beyond the scope of your intellectual capacities, please refrain from having your minds —what there is of such — unnecessarily and dangerously led into anti-social acts of cruelty and destruction by the frenzied instigations of that Stone Age assemblage known as the fans, who will only see what they want to see and will, time and time again, convict such whistle blowing asshole and absolute moron as myself of the most abject stupidity to fan, player and coach alike, such coach, who feels it his responsibility to badger and provoke the nerd in stripes, your coach red, and your coach white, duty bound to protect your interests against my sightless eyes and empty skull. This, of course, could be no further from the truth due to the fact that all these fictions become fact because the human animal – and animals we are so proven to be at events like this – is not ready for this game of basketball, not you red, nor you white, nor all the hateful fans and coaches and pubescent, suckable, Lolita cheerleaders, no, not mature enough, hip enough, mellow enough, grown up enough, not far enough evolved to be allowed to participate in such participations. But we are brave – if nothing else positive can be said of all this, at least we can say we are brave. Brave enough to at least try once again, hoping that some degree of sane, civilized behavior will be in evidence, enough so that no one will be mentally or physically scarred for life from what we are dauntingly going to proceed with momentarily. But I'm not done! And while I'm on the matter, please find it within your hearts, or lungs, or testicles, or whatever, to permit one full game to go by without the threat of physical abuse to my person within during, or without after the game, which also implies an absence of smoldering, hateful glances in my direction each time you are caught bending the rules, for I can assure you that having been outscored by your opponent, in case you haven't heard, means you have lost, and neither I nor my colleagues will have been the reason for such defeat, though I'm quite certain such excuse – and pathetic, childish excuse it is – will be put into the minutes of this meeting even though 20, 30, or even more tallies separate victory from defeat. But one can never lose hope, even in its most microscopic quantity, hope for a smile and handshake after the game, hope for some small appreciation for the impossible task undertaken by us, the designated idiots, for having been courageous enough to swim against the pounding tide of human ignorance so that you red, and you white, could more fully enjoy your adolescence with a clean, hard fought, sporting game of basketball, meant to be part of the well rounded education our tax dollars are so vainly invested in. Any questions?

While Edie submerged herself in the reading, Sam continued to swing on the playground apparatus. From time to time, he would steal a glance in her direction, trying to measure her appreciation of the work. Her concentration seemed intense and slight giggles and random smiles punctuated her attention. When she had finally finished reading, she folded the aging piece of paper and got up. She walked over to the swings, smiled, and sat on the swing next to him. He stopped swinging. She gave him the piece of paper and he tucked it into his pants pocket.

They sat for awhile. The clean pop of rebounding tennis balls from the nearby courts invaded the atmosphere. What a pleasant sound it was.

Edie laughed lightly and shook her head. "Pubescent, suckable, Lolita cheerleaders. You know, you could probably get away with everything else, but that's what they'd crucify you for."

Sam smiled and swung lightly on the swings. The announcer at the softball field was asking for the lineups for the evening's last game. The woman's league was playing that night and judging from the spandex pants and form fitting tee shirts, strutting your stuff seemed as important as playing the game. It reminded Sam as to why he was there.

"Yeah," he said, as he continued swinging easily, "you can drop bombs on defenseless people all over the world, but just have one out of wedlock blow job and they won't let you be the Municipal Dog Catcher."

They laughed heartily, shook their heads in mutual resignation, and headed out of the park into the night.

Chapter 22

An Important Decision

They left the park from the opposite direction from where they had entered. Once again, they found themselves immersed in the darkened streets of the Old Barrio. The dense tropical canopy insinuated itself from all sides – mahogany trees, banyan-ficus trees, sapodillas with their thick cover of smallish green leaves dotted with the hard brown balls of fruit ripening by the thousands. Even in the dead of winter, this was a lush vegetable environment, with parasitical vines in a Baskin & Robbins assortment of colors and forms climbing and clinging to the mature trees lining the streets. Absent any human intervention, it wouldn't be long before this perpetual vegetable onslaught would bury and destroy all that had been built here. Coconut palms, one of the true signature plants of the tropics, were always in evidence somewhere, silhouetted against the night sky.

"Sam, I'm cold."

Edie had not expected to be out at this time without having returned home. Her loose green blouse had been fine for her afternoon stroll, but as the evening wore on it had become insufficient. She was walking with her arms crossed over her chest and her head, seeking some kind of shelter, buried in her shoulders. Suddenly, a good natured blond lab came running up to Sam, wagging his tail, doggy laughing, gently putting his paws on his hips in a happy greeting.

"Hi'ya Beau, how ya' doin' ol' buddy?" Sam knelt down

and let the dog smear his face with doggy kisses. He gently pushed him to the ground and began rubbing his tummy, much to the joy of his canine friend, who lay flat on his back, doggy paws flailing, grunting and squirming with glee. As our hero rubbed and rubbed, he went into a kind of mantra: "he's the tummy rubbin'est dog, the tummy rubbin'est dog, the tummy rubbin'est dog –"

"Is that your dog?"

He rubbed a bit longer and made Beau get up. "Nah, this is Beau, he's my buddy." The dog continued to wiggle his butt. Sam smacked him good-naturedly on his rump, just above his brownish-white tail. He spoke to the dog one more time. "He's a tummy rubbin' dog."

Edie stood with her arms crossed, obviously cold in the night air. Sam realized he'd been rude. "I'm sorry, you said you were cold." She nodded. "Look, I live on this block. My house is just a few doors away." Sam felt a slight pang of guilt, not having let on that he was kind of heading in this direction, hoping to perhaps entice her –entice? It sounded so, what? –Dishonest? "I can get you a jacket or something."

They started walking. Beau trailed along behind. "Is that how you know the dog?"

"I've known Beau since he was a puppy. He's always had a good home –he's very friendly."

Edie knelt down and stroked the dog's back. She put her head close to his snout. Within a few seconds he was swabbing her with wet kisses. "He's beautiful."

The block was a typical Old Barrio landscape of Victorian homes flanking a tree-lined street. Most of the trees were big, mature mahogany trees, planted during the Depression as part of the WPA's attempt to put people back to work. Quick growing shade trees was the idea, and it had worked to perfection. Sam lived in a big two-story house, both floors equipped with a porch facing the street. Like so many of the beautiful old houses, it had been converted into 2, 3 or even more apartments. Sam lived on the bottom floor.

"Would you like to come in?" said Sam timidly, still unsettled by his secret subterfuge meant to get her near his house. Edie continued playing with the dog as she considered the offer. For some inexplicable reason, this seemed to be an important decision. Entering his house would break the rhythm, indicating some form of game change. It would signal a new phase of – what? Silly as it seemed, she wasn't ready to enter his house, to see how he lived, if he was sloppy, neat, whatever. She wasn't ready for that kind of intimacy. "Edie?" he repeated impatiently, "would you like to come in while I get you a jacket?"

"Oh, sorry," she stuttered, turning her gaze away from the dog and towards Sam. "No, I'll just wait here with Beau."

Sam looked at her momentarily, wondering once again if this were all just a waste of time. His confidence had been shaken. Turning abruptly, he hurried into the house.

Edie continued to play with the dog as she waited. The dim sound of rock music trickled into the street. It was coming from the house next door to Sam's, a similar 2-story structure. It was music she had heard before but could not identify – maybe Pearl Jam, or some other rehash of the same old thing, even if they did call it "new wave." Edie had often tried to find the "new" in this wave of rock music, but it always ended up sounding like the wave she'd been brought up on, only a bit more tired, more used up, more –

nothing. The silhouette of a young girl working in the kitchen caught our lady's eye. Denise-of-the-perfect-butt?

Sam returned carrying a light blue windbreaker. Being that our hero was not much taller than the object of his pursuit, the length and sleeves were not too bad, but his more masculine bulk left Edie swimming inside it. In a way, it really was "cute," as if Sam had just given his high school sweetheart his letter jacket to wear. They laughed as she modeled the garment.

"What do you think?" she said, as if she were walking in a fashion show in Milan or Paris.

"Beautiful. Gucci, Armani, Walmart." They laughed once again and headed off into the night. Another inning had been completed. The game went on.

Chapter 23

Does it Make Sense?

Our couple began walking once again. Where were they going? "Sam, where are we going?"

Before Sam could answer, the faint pounding of something resembling a gigantic, universal heartbeat, began insinuating itself into the environment. They listened as it got closer – *boomp, boomp, boomp* – closer, louder – **boomp, boomp** – 10 seconds later the thump was just about upon them. A late model pickup truck, obviously the focal point of some adolescent male's life, turned onto the block. It was painted in a glittering shade of purple and there was an accessory on the underside that lit the street under the vehicle in a similar shade of purple. By now, in addition to the pulsating bass thump, the lyrics of a rap song could be heard. It seemed to be some kind of ode to filthy language, with the words fuck, cunt, suck, cock, nigger and other assorted elements of the most depraved street jargon occupying the bulk of its verbal communication.

The purple extravaganza passed them with all the subtlety of a tornado. The license plate on its rear bumper was lit like a used car lot, with purple lights moving around the plate.

As had been the case earlier in our story when a Harley had interrupted their serenity, Edie closed her eyes and covered her ears. She held this pose for about 20 seconds. Finally, she dropped her hands and breathed deeply.

"Do the words offend you?" asked Sam.

The pick up truck had sped off to who knows where. Remarkably, the thump could still be heard. "No Sam, the language has nothing to do with it. Who knows, there might even be something creative there. That's not what I question." The vehicle could have been two or three blocks away, but our pair was downwind and the thump could still be heard.

"Amazing," said Sam, "imagine being inside the car itself."

"The intellectual content of any attempt at creation," said Edie seriously, "is never something I would put a leash on. I might disagree with its message, but it would never offend me. What offends me is the incivility of what these young people are doing. Nobody's recreation should be allowed to invade someone else's tranquility – or happiness. A society that sits back and does not demand this kind of respect from minds that are still in the process of learning right from wrong, is losing its concept of civility."

By now the thump had finally moved off into someone else's tranquility. Sam looked at Edie and smiled. "You know, I love it when you get serious like that. Sometimes I think I'm the only person left who ever gets serious about anything. I frequently find myself annoying people when I get serious – it's like they don't want to hear it. Shut up, watch the game, pass the beer."

Edie sighed and almost imperceptibly shook her head. "I guess you always have to know who your audience is, but I think there's something important here in this truck thump business. Our culture's whole rhetoric, its code words – I don't know –" she seemed confused, unsure.

Sam interjected, "I think I know what you mean. It's like this 'in your face' attitude is getting out of control. Compete, win, vanquish. Don't give a fuck about anyone else, be all that you can be, me, me, look at me."

"I agree Sam, but –" she seemed a bit unsatisfied with his remarks, "– it's not exactly what I mean. As a culture we seem to have lost track of the fact that finding a way to reconcile –" she shook her head in frustration. "I'm just not getting it."

The sound of another thumping vehicle could dimly be heard in the distance, but it was not heading their way. They laughed as they listened to it fade off in the night. Their odyssey resumed. After a few steps, Edie stopped. Sam continued on for a moment before noticing her absence. He turned around just as she said, "It's like, we've begun to value vanquishing each other more than loving each other. It's like, everything our culture glorifies is a call to confrontation, is a challenge, is a chance to see who is better – as if subduing someone is more fulfilling than loving someone – Oh Christ, listen to that shit."

"No Edie, don't ever be ashamed to say it. Don't ever be ashamed."

The haunting sound of a Klee Klee hawk wafted through the trees and over their heads – *klee, klee* –Sam was so glad to hear them again. *Klee, klee, klee –*

Edie was still wrapped up in her own thoughts. "Did any of that actually make sense?"

Sam listened for the hawk's soothing sound, but it had probably flown off. "Does it make sense?" He pondered the question for a moment. "Well, it doesn't make mathematical sense or scientific sense, there is no algebraic equation that proves it —but yeah, it makes a lot of sense."

Klee, klee – there it was, as if it were affirming our hero's thoughts.

Chapter 24

Steve Forbes

*S*am and Edie continued walking. Where were they going? "Sam, where are we going?"

"Didn't we already decide that?" said Sam, feeling that strange feeling of déjà vu.

Edie was not quite sure. If they had, she couldn't remember where it was they were going. They had now reached a more principle street and, for reasons unknown, had turned onto it. Although there was not much traffic by this time of day, a lesser flow of vehicles was still circulating. Most of the small businesses that flanked the street had already closed; a second hand furniture store, an electronics repair shop, a paint store, a bicycle shop. The small supermarket that served the locals in the neighborhood was also closed, but a few last minute shoppers – cat food, bread, toilet paper – were still checking out at the registers. Although this was a commercial artery, it was a genuine place, far enough from the downtown tourist hustle to not be infected by the tourism monster. A traffic light on the next corner kept the rhythm of the night.

"Well Sam, if we've already decided where we are going, you tell me?"

When they had reached the corner with the traffic light, they stopped and gave thought. A Laundromat-snack bar sent forth a shower of neon light into the muted light of the street. A smattering of people were robotically going about their laundry chores – folding clothes, impatiently waiting for the washers and dryers to complete their cycles, mindlessly reading newspapers, trying to get it done. The snack bar was closed but the lights were still on as the crew cleaned the long day's accumulated muck from the floors, refrigerators and espresso machines. One of the Mexicans who ran the business was dragging 2 overflowing cans of garbage out to the curb. By 5 o'clock the next morning, the whole cycle would start again. God, thought Sam, the hours these people put in.

Edie seemed to be reading his mind. "Boy," she said, "the American Dream. Woo!"

"I suppose you have to go through lots of nightmare before it begins to be a dream. As long as there is still a third world, the dream will always be there."

Although this was the place where Sam did his own laundry, he stared into it as if he were examining it for the first time. His curiosity seemed out of place.

"What are you looking at Sam?"

He seemed surprised by her interjection. He turned and said, "When I was in college I used to play a game with Laundromats. I suppose you could call it stealing, but by then I already knew that stealing is an esoteric concept that can be defined by whoever's self interest is in play."

Edie cut in, "OK, let's just say you were providing yourself with a sounder fiscal foundation to cruise through life with –like what Steve Forbes does."

"Exactly!" The ham in Sam was about to break loose. "Financial security and all that, babies, weddings, college educations, a lawn to mow and a train to catch. Dishwashers, freezers, washers and dryers, a TV for the den, the kids' and the master bedroom. Charcoal briquettes, microwaves, video games, iPads, smart phones, dumb phones, Facebook and Twitter, can we find a baby sitter? Avis, Hertz, a week in Jamaica; Cancun, San Juan, discount flights and 6 days and 7 nights. Credit, gold and platinum cards; IRA's, CEO's, DDT's, MRI's, HMO's and aluminum siding, where are all those roaches hiding? I'm here to fix the boiler, paint the house and wax the floor, and oh, yeah, antiques, carpeting, drapes, tune ups and anti-freeze, hospitals and heart attacks, hemorrhoids, nose jobs, braces, dentists, beauty parlors, face lifts, health spas, and gee, watch out for cholesterol so you can live to use your skis, racquets, clubs, slices, hooks, hacks, divots and handicaps, kayaks, helmets and canoes, gizmos made to play the blues. And oh, have I got a headache, Advil, Tylenol, Motrin and Bayer, I'm going crazy being a player. Cameras, coolers, soft drinks, hot dogs, mustard, relish, station wagons and SUV's; Christmas, honeymoons, anniversaries, birthdays, daddy, daddy, I want, I need, what am I getting? Sears, Walmart, Penny's, Bloomingdale's, Foot Locker, Nike, Reebok, Michael, Jeter and Shaq –"

"Sam?" Edie pulled gently on his arm. "Sam?"

"Oh," he said, returning to our own galaxy. She's touching me, he thought. "Sometimes I get carried away."

"That's OK, I think it's cute." Sam looked at her with that brooding quality she had now become familiar with. "OK, OK, you're not cute."

"Where were we?"

"You were explaining how you stole money from Laundromats."

"Oh yeah."

Chapter 25

Ready to Die

"OK, the plan," said Sam, "cop a little change, buddy can you spare just enough for somethin' t'eat, so forth and blah, blah, blah. Let's face it, there's a healthy segment of our freedom loving society free enough to engage in such practices. By the way, though I am the originator of this technique, I have never used this plan for my own enrichment, oh for shame no. The social class from which I was spawned frowns upon such behavior, though we have our own ways of stealing; wholesale-retail, investments, brokers, financial advisors and such, 'spin', marketing, third class mail, spam – much more respectable –"

"Sam, that's a hard sell, don't you think?"

"At this point, I'd say trying to sell anyone on decent, respectable, honorable behavior in our society is a hard sell. But when you get to the marrow of it all, everyone is just hustling everyone else in this land of liberty and objective news swindling. I think when we talk of liberty or freedom in this country, we are now talking about the liberty to cheat and swindle each other – Gillette Gods and such. You're the one who came up with that, don't you remember?"

"Hmm, I think you may have just sold me."

"Eureka."

They trudged on through the night. A block past the traffic light they turned onto a residential street. The tropical canopy engulfed them again. The vegetation murmured secretly in the light air and the insect hum unconsciously invaded the endless spin of the planet.

"But Sam, if you didn't keep the money, what did you do with it?"

"I would give it to homeless people. I was playing at being Robin Hood."

"Sam, you're a real humanitarian."

Our man shrugged and blew air through his mouth, as if to mock the statement. "Nowadays, I never give money to panhandlers. They are lost causes, people who our society has eaten up and spit out. They're not going to do anything positive with the money anyway. Nowadays, I concern myself with the broad picture, with trying to convince people to abandon their Gillette Gods, to try and build a world without so many demoralized and defeated people." He put his hands over his eyes and shook his head. "Holy cow, listen to that shit."

The roles were now reversed. "No Sam, don't ever be ashamed to say it." They smiled at each other and moved on. "So what is this Laundromat change hustling technique?"

"What you do is hang around a Laundromat with a small sack of clothes, just to make it look right. Almost all such places have a few machines that are not working, usually with an 'out of order' sign on it or with the coin slots taped up. You surreptitiously remove the warning and put some clothes in the machine, at which point the heist is prepared to yield results. You then seek out the low life in charge, usually the creature with all the keys dangling by his side who may be dozing in front of the establishment's TV. When he can be identified, you politely inform him that you've lost your money in such and such machine. He, with all the dignity of his hierarchy in the grand scheme of things, will proceed to examine the machine in question. He will then shake his head, swearing to himself that this machine had been marked. You will now be handed anywhere from $2.00 to $3.00, depending on the greed of the establishment and the cost of living of its geographic location. Take the money and mumble something about shitty machines. Don't be too polite. Act as if you are proceeding to another machine. When the low life goes back to dozing in front of Vin Diesel – this won't take long – you're out'a there. Pretty good, huh?"

"Not bad. Perhaps this low life thievery is your true vocation?"

"Hey, maybe so," said Sam as they continued walking. "If I had only been born in some fried chicken-hip hop ghetto – I could have been a panhandling star of poverty instead of this stumbling, ill-conceived escapee from the American Dream, never quite sure of my role, spouting these over-brained verbosities in futility."

"C'mon Sam, where's that man who ripped off his tie and stuffed it into his pocket? Do I detect some insecurity here?"

As they trekked on, a silence fell over them, as if they were taking a time out to mull it over in their minds. Just what did Sam feel about himself? He certainly felt no remorse in leaving the "old country," as he called his previous life, but had he really found something he could truly hold onto in its place? No doubt it had been a great adventure, something he wouldn't have missed for anything. "Insecure?" he said insecurely. "Does anyone really know exactly what they want from this life? Are people like Derek Jeter or Jay Leno or – let's just say the people we hold out as the most successful in our society – are they always the happiest, the most fulfilled? Isn't there something disappointing about everyone's life?"

Edie could not help herself. "How about Hugh Hefner?"

Sam broke out laughing, a snorting, whooping kind of out of control laughter that was contagious. When the two of them had calmed down a bit, our boy shook his head and said, "well, if there is someone who has not been disappointed, I'd bet it's him."

Edie shook her head and smiled. "You gorillas are all the same."

In spite of the merriment produced by Edie's sense of humor, the subject matter was worthy of respect. The journey went on in silence, the tranquility of the Old Barrio night engulfing them. The mundane noises of humans living in close concert with each other – an occasional car horn, a door slamming, an errant TV sound from within a house – did not interfere with their mental machinations.

"I suppose," Edie finally broke the silence, "it's very hard to live up to the standard of happiness sold to us by the objective news swindlers and the whole commercial sound machine that creates our culture's concept of happiness. This is supposed to be the happiest place in the history of the planet. In our society, it has become obligatory to be happy. There is an unending quest to be happier than we've ever been before. In fact, we're supposed to be happier tomorrow than we are today. Who could ever live up to such expectations?"

Sam nodded in agreement. "At least I've objectively

chosen my own form of insecurity. It may be easier to live with that. For those who've been led by the nose in pursuit of the American Dream, the insecurity must be even greater. They've invested so much in it. If it turns out not to be all it's cracked up to be —that's real disappointment." They walked on in silence once again, perhaps for a minute. "Maybe I should have been a child of the ratted tenement wilderness?" he continued. "Who knows, I might have made it to the top; fire engine red Lincoln Continental with fat white wall tires, girls to pimp, drugs to sell —now there's a man not insecure about anything. He's even ready to die." They walked on mutely a few moments more. "Ah, the injustice of it all."

"Justice?" said our fair lady, "now there's something I've lost hope in. Karma maybe – but man made justice? I don't think so?"

"Sometimes Edie, I like to play at justice. Would you like to play?'

"How do you play?"

Chapter 26

Pablito's Cuban Mix

As they wandered on, Sam explained the game. "Actually, it's a very simple game that momentarily gives those of us with no power to judge anything a chance to vent our frustrations. Either of the participants can decide to bring up any alleged criminal they want and the other participant comes up with a verdict. But the verdict should be something to try and rehabilitate the criminal, something he or she should learn. You go first. Who do you want to go before the dubious inquisitors of justice?"

"Gosh," said Edie, "who amongst us couldn't be condemned for something?"

"True," said our man, "but that's the point of the game. Even so called good guys are guilty. If it makes you feel better go for some real transgressors; go for some big fish, some real players. Maybe later on we can go for some good guys."

The insects hummed, the cats fought, the foliage rustled in the tropical winter night. Stars dotted the roof of life. Edie wrinkled her forehead and tried to find someone to prosecute. "OK, how about –"

"Hold it!" Sam assumed a formal, affected posture and solemnly trumpeted the following: "Here ye, here ye, the People's Progressive Unaggressive Laid Back Semi Stoned Home Grown Revolutionary Non Institutionary Mango Mellowed Court is now in session. You may all rise, but, if you've a mind to, you may all sit. You may all diddle your neighbors if you'd like. Suck yourself off for all I care, no matter; this court is now in session."

Edie was laughing. "OK, now we are official. Can we proceed?"

"Yes, now that we have sanctified, ritualized, legitimized – yes, this court is now worthy of respect."

"Are you done?"

"Yes, proceed."

"OK, let's start with Bill Clinton."

"Ahh, good one. What could be more fashionable than to judge an ex leader of the world's only super – what was that word you used – schmegeg, shmo –?"

"You mean 'schmeggegy'?"

"Right, right – of the world's only super schmeggegy power?" Sam did not have to think too long. "OK, I've got it –"

"Wow, that was quick."

"We already touched upon this subject back in the park. Bill Clinton will be sent to re-education camp where he will learn that dropping bombs on defenseless people is more shameful than his fellatial escapades with political groupies."

"Excellent Sam. You mean like 'less bombs and more boners?"

Once again, Edie had him laughing with her surprising sense of humor. "Right on sister. I guess 'make love not war' still works for me. In truth, I think we could substitute any president's name and come up with the same verdict."

Edie was even harsher. "Or how about 'the American people'? Couldn't we just send the majority of the population to re-education camp where they would learn that dropping bombs on defenseless people is more shameful than – just about anything?"

"I won't argue with that."

"OK Sam, how about one for me?"

"Well, as long as you started it – do you remember Kenneth Starr?"

"Sure – the Torquemada of presidential morality."

"Go to it – Kenneth Starr."

She contorted her face in exaggerated, mock concentration. Sam laughed and thought this girl was the 'cutest' thing he'd ever laid eyes on. My God – "Sam, a question."

"Shoot."

"Is there capital punishment in this jurisdiction?"

Sam sighed and shrugged his shoulders. "Well, with regard to Kenneth Starr, that's a good question." He pondered for a moment. A car drove by with the radio turned up, the DJ ranting about some contest or giveaway. Maybe, he thought, he'd like to kill that driver playing the radio so loud; or maybe the DJ with his adolescent rants; or maybe half the people he crossed paths with. "No, I think not. I've never been an eye for an eye kind of guy – an eye for a finger, maybe."

"OK then, Kenneth Starr; he will be sent to re-education camp where he will learn that nerds are not qualified to judge sexual improprieties."

"Perfect. That guy needs to get a little." Who doesn't, he thought, as soon as he'd said it?

"I'm sure he can afford it. My chance." Sam nodded. "OK, how about Rupert Murdoch?"

"Wow," Sam whistled lowly, "we really are going for big fish now."

"Well, if there really is something wrong with this mangy world of Gillette Gods and such, he's had as much to do with it as anyone."

"Hmmm," murmured our hero as he sat in judgment. Rupert Murdoch – Sam had often thought, in his mind fucking cavilations, that this one man had had more to do with what was wrong on this earth than anyone else. Edie's remark hit him right in the bull's eye. Rupert Murdoch. Where was he? Where did he hang out? It was as if he were some kind of universal presence that existed in everything – but did not exist at all. You could feel him but you could never see or touch him. Rupert Murdoch was almost something metaphysical, abstract – like God. "Rupert Murdoch –" he continued to think about it.

"C'mon Sam, he's just another human being."

"Is he?" He went on thinking. Suddenly, something caught his attention. "Wow! Did you see it?"

"See what?"

"The shooting star." He pointed to where it had burned its way through the sky. "Maybe it was a warning from Rupert. Like hey, don't take my name in vane."

They both laughed. "C'mon Sam, Rupert Murdoch."

"OK, Rupert Murdoch: he will be sent to re-education camp where he will learn that if there really is one God, he's not It."

Edie seemed unsatisfied. "Makes you long for the death penalty, doesn't it?"

"Yeah –" Sam shrugged and smiled sadly, "but we cannot stoop to his level. We are better than that."

She ambiguously affirmed his assertion and left it at that. They walked on. "OK, give me one Sam."

They were now passing a Cuban grocery store that stayed open late. Everyone who'd lived in town for a long time had lived, at one time or another, in this neighborhood; in fact, Edie lived close by. The same family had run the business for more than 50 years. It was an anomaly in a residential neighborhood, something that had managed to survive simpler times. The little store specialized in Cuban products like canned papaya slices, malta soft drinks, latino spices and the like. There was also a "to go" kitchen – *para llevar* in Spanish – serving such Cuban delicacies as "bollos," home made bean soups, and excellent Cuban sandwiches. Pablito's Cuban mix was reputed amongst the best on the island. At the lunch hour there was always a crowd of workers from the electric company or public works, many of whose employees were Lenos who had grown up in this neighborhood but still came back to eat with Pablo – milling about outside, gustily devouring their midday meal. It was the kind of place truly worth visiting that no tourist ever saw. Sam thought how ironic it was that a tourist never saw anything.

"You know Edie, if my sustenance clock is not mistaken, there's a good chance I might be hungry. How about you?"

"I could eat."

They went in.

Chapter 27

A Well Played Game

The store was located on a corner and the front door was flanked on each side by a pair of uncomfortable old benches, 2 of which faced one street and 2 more facing the other. In stark contrast to the midday bustle, the corner was a quiet place at this time of day, with an occasional car, bicycle or pedestrian passing by. Some last minute customers seeking the day's last buchi, which was the local's way of saying an espresso, drifted in and out.

Our couple sat on one of the benches, eagerly eating their impromptu meals. Sam was having a hierba, which was a Cuban mix without the ham. It was a light offering featuring lettuce, tomato, pickle, and a thin slice of excellent queso blanco – what the gringos call Swiss cheese – all served on a steamed piece of Cuban bread. The Cubans used a small device which looked like something a dry cleaner would use to press a shirt that kept the bread fresh all day. The steam was just enough to slightly melt the thin slice of cheese. He accompanied it with a bag of plantain chips and a coke. Edie was eating an order of bollos, which were golf ball size dumplings of deep fried garbanzo beans. She had opted for a bag of potato chips and washed it all down with Perrier Water. She had also purchased 2 plastic strands of Slim Jims, which she had filed away in her waist purse.

"You know Edie," said Sam as he chewed on a plantain chip, "I never figured you as a Slim Jim kind of person."

Edie laughed and slightly gagged on a mouthful of bollo. She cleared her throat with a swig of water. "No, no," she said, dabbing the side of her mouth with a napkin, "it's for my dog Pancho. He loves them, you'll see."

Her words hit Sam like a religious revelation. "I will?" he said hopefully.

Our fair lady realized her *faux pas*. She bit into her next bollo and tried to rectify the situation, speaking with her mouth half full. "Sometime or other, I guess."

Sam frowned and took another bite of his sandwich. He could feel a slight tingle in his spine, which eventually found its way to his more private areas. He was on the verge of being aroused and was reminded of the high stakes game currently under way. He suddenly felt impatient.

"Edie, do we have any idea as to how this game is going?"

"Well," she said, as she swallowed her food, "I'd say it's a well played game in the middle innings, good pitching, certainly a game worth watching no matter what happens. It could go either way."

This did not particularly please our man. He looked out into the street, gazing at nothing in particular, that now familiar brooding quality evident once again.

"C'mon," she said, in an effort to break the tension, "let's play some more at 'justice'."

He snapped out of it. "OK."

Chapter 28

Tyson and Holyfield

By now our duo had just about finished their meals. Sam was polishing off his last few plantain chips and Edie was down to her last bollo. They had both prudently saved enough of their drinks to wash it all down with.

"Whose turn is it Sam?"

"I think I need some dessert." He got up and brushed some crumbs off his sweatshirt. "Do you want something?"

"How 'bout a Hershey bar."

He disappeared into the store, returning in less than 30 seconds. He handed her one of the 2 chocolate bars he had bought.

"I don't care whose turn it is," he said, "I have one for you." He sat down and unwrapped his candy bar. "Judging from your baseball analogy just a moment ago, it seems you might be a fan, no?"

By now Edie was daintily biting into her first delicate wedge of chocolate. "Hmmm, I love chocolate." She chewed and swallowed, wallowing in the delight of the culinary treat. "Hmm –" she smacked her lips with exaggeration. Sam laughed. "I have a couple of older brothers I used to trail along behind. We used to come in from south Jersey to see the Phillies play."

"Do you know who 'El Duque' is?"

"You mean the Cuban who ended up pitching for the Yankees?"

"Right. I've always considered him one of the greatest pitching artists I've ever seen."

"You seem to know a lot about it."

"I've played some ball."

"You want me to judge him?"

"Sure, everyone is guilty of something. Didn't you say that?"

"OK, I'll try, but he seems like a pretty good guy to me. My oldest brother played college ball at Temple University and he loved him too."

They continued eating their dessert as Edie thought it over. Every so often one of them would punctuate their chewing with a gulp of liquid. Edie imperceptibly began to shake her head, not being able to accuse "El Duque" of anything.

"C'mon Edie – El Duque."

"Quiet," she said sharply, "I'm thinking." She began thinking about sports in general; the greed, the big salaries, the high-ticket prices, the strikes – "I've got it! El Duque: he will be sent to re-education camp –"

Sam cut in. "That's kind of funny, don't you think? I'm sure they tried to educate and re-educate this guy a thousand times back in Cuba. He'd have probably been Mike Tyson or something if he had been born here. A born rebel."

"Sam, maybe you're right, but you are out of order. Can I proceed with the verdict?"

"Sorry." He ate his last piece of chocolate.

"El Duque: he will be sent to re-education camp where he will learn that what he was paid in Cuba for playing baseball was the correct amount."

"Beautiful. Right on sister." Sam took his last gulp of coke, gathered the loose papers and napkins, and stuffed it all in the paper bag it came in. "Really, El Duque and the boys who play today in any sport can go on strike all they want. It's my garbage man I really need."

Having finished off their food and drink, they say contentedly in the crisp night air. A couple on bicycles leisurely rode by, waving to them as they passed. Our couple returned the salute. What a beautiful night it was.

"OK Sam, I've got another one for you."

"Lay it on me," he said happily; glad she was into his game.

"Mike Tyson. You brought him up, give me a verdict."

The ancient bench was not constructed with any orthopedic philosophy in mind. Sam could feel his back resisting the lumpy contours of the old planks they were sitting on. As he thought about Mike Tyson he tried to rectify the liquid posture he had fallen into. He stretched his arms over his head, straightened his legs, and eventually fell into a more upright sitting position.

"C'mon Sam, quit stalling."

"Take it easy."

"What's so hard? The guy eats people, abuses women – "

"I know, I know –" Sam continued to muddle it over. Yeah, yeah, Mike Tyson – he had become one of America's official bad guys. He was someone we were supposed to frown upon institutionally. He was an example to your kids of how you were not supposed to be. And yet – Sam always found himself sympathizing with him. He always found himself not liking his great nemesis, Evander Holyfield.

Holyfield had been made the official good guy, the religious guy with a stable of illegitimate kids. Sam could smell something sour here, a media fabrication, a crock of crap propagated by the status quo.

"Mike Tyson: not guilty."

"You're kidding?" Edie was surprised.

Sam sat silently for awhile, lightly twisting and stretching his lower back. He gazed into the distance in a sightless stare that was almost angry. Fuck'em, he thought, he didn't buy their CNN bullshit. He didn't hate Fidel, or Saddam – he didn't hate Moamar or Chavez. True, he didn't look upon men of this nature as positive saviors, but were they any better or worse than our guys? Everyone has their own particular agenda based upon their own particular self-interest. There was enough blood to go around on all sides. Good guys? Bad guys? No, he thought, I don't think so. The practitioners of the Nike-Nasdaq horseshit him and Edie lived under had no right to tell anyone who was good or bad. He wondered if these mangy days of Gillette Gods would ever end. Would we ever break on through to the other side? "Jim Morrison," he whispered to himself.

"Who?"

He snapped out of it. "No, no, I was just –"

"Why do you think Tyson is not guilty?"

"If there is one thing that truly scares America, it's an out front person, someone who doesn't hide behind an image, someone who doesn't try to market themselves. America has grown comfortable with bullshit. When somebody comes along who doesn't give them bullshit, it puts everyone uptight. Mike Tyson is not bullshit."

"That could be true," replied Edie, "but does he give

anyone something positive to replace it with?"

Our hero stared blankly into the darkened street. The dim sound of a motorcycle revving up could be heard leaking through the tropical vegetable screen. "Maybe not, but he's still not guilty. Tyson knows who he is and where he came from. He knows something is wrong. He knows that somehow or other, he and whoever he represents –and he represents a lot of people just like him – have been given a raw deal. His instincts are good. He lashes out at the right people, the right things – but his intellect is not well enough developed to give himself or anyone else any answers. His justifiable anger can't find its proper course. It's an anger that constantly overflows its banks and ends up doing damage."

Edie tried being objective. As a woman, Tyson's run-ins with her gender had naturally encouraged her antipathy. She leaned forward, her chin resting in her hand as she mulled it over. "Something like Cassius Clay without the charm and grace."

"Something like that." His face continued to brood, chiseled in a stony, sightless stare. His dark brows seemed to be clamping down tighter over his deep-set eyes. A vertical wrinkle, the result of years of cerebral overtime, cut a deep path between them. "Not guilty," he repeated.

Chapter 29

Downtown

Edie took her last swig of Perrier and, much as Sam had done, put it in her paper bag along with the napkins and paper container her bollos had come in. By now it was a bit after 10 o'clock.

The lights in the little Cuban grocery store went off behind them. Pablo's son Joey, who now did most of the work in the store, appeared in the doorway, ready to lock up for the night. He noticed our pair sitting on the bench. "Nice night, eh?"

"Beautiful," said our pair, sounding like a rehearsed duet. They shrugged with embarrassment. Joey smiled.

"How was the food?" asked Joey.

"Horrible," said Sam, "But I just got back from Kabul where I was held hostage for 3 years. I was hungry."

Everyone laughed. "Well, have a good night."

Our couple nodded and Joey disappeared inside the store, locking the door behind him. It was time to move on. Transition moments such as this were the most dangerous moments. It meant they had to decide something. The dreaded awkward silence was upon them. They filled the void with trivial actions; straightening clothes, stretching bodies, disposal of garbage in the nearby receptacles. Once again, a car drove by with its radio turned up: "**downtown, things will be great when you're downtown, everything's waiting for you –**" Sam thought it odd that a person listening to such old music would have the radio up so loud. Some people never grow up, he thought – or maybe they never got tired of living. Had he gotten tired of living?

By now they were only a few blocks from the downtown area. Neither one of them, except for work or some other essential reason – perhaps a "snowbird" relative or friend down for a visit – ventured into the jaws of this tourist area very much. But this was a special occasion, thought Sam, maybe they should treat it as such. "Wha'd'ya'say Edie, how 'bout if we check out the bullshit downtown?"

She shrugged noncommittally, barely muttering an "OK."

Good enough for me, he thought. Their Odyssey was renewed.

Chapter 30

Close to Nature

They walked on in mute mental exhaustion. Residues of the awkward silence were still clinging to them. Sam told himself to relax. He noticed a mature mango tree – one of the best producers in town, at least over the last few years – lit by the beige light of a street lamp. In about two to three months it would be hung heavy with a kidney shaped bounty of red-green, grenade sized fruit – or even bigger. One of the most beautiful spectacles in nature was a mango tree hung lustily with its sweet tasting produce. Most people in the temperate climate of the developed world were unaware that the mango was the most eaten fruit in the world. The tree was flowering with zest, showing all the promise that was yet to come. There were even a few golf ball sized babies beginning to appear on its branches.

"Do you like mangos Edie?"

"I do, but I'm allergic to them. Can you believe it?"

"It's not that uncommon."

The journey went on. The crisis had not been totally averted. Sam felt the need to rescue the moment, probably unnecessarily, but his desire for this girl, his chance at something he hadn't had for so long, had him in an insecure dither. He needed to say something, anything.

"Is there anyone else you might want brought to justice?" He felt as if a fly had just flown in his mouth.

"No, no," she sounded tired, bored, "I think we've had

enough of that. In truth, I don't feel righteous enough to judge anyone. I try to defend myself from the madness, but I can't judge. My approach is to forgive them for they know not what they do. I think we have good old J.C. to thank for that one."

"Yes, and one of his better ones, don't you think?" He felt relieved. They seemed to have come out of it naturally. Relax Sam, relax. He went on. "I once had the pleasure of being deserted by a lover – this was years ago, when I first came here – who, in lieu of me, had fallen in love with Jesus. Quite a put down, don't you think? He's been dead for 2,000 years."

"Maybe by now," our lady said sarcastically, "she's left Jesus for Casper the Friendly Ghost?" She paused for a moment and added, "or maybe she hadn't found out she was going to be a lesbian?" Hmmph, she thought to herself, at least she's making it with someone. That's more than she could say for herself.

Sam thought about it. "More likely. Gee, I hope it wasn't me." He shuddered as he pondered the idea. "In any event, needless to say, I bounced back."

"Needless to say."

Sam could not help but think back on that experience. At the time it was a crushing blow. He shook his head and laughed lightly.

"What's so funny?" she wanted to know.

He laughed a bit more. He was laughing at himself. "I was madly in love with that girl." A sad smile appeared on his face as he continued shaking his head. "You know, making love to her was like making love to a stage prop. She really wasn't into it, but it made me want her even more."

"Did you have something to prove, your ego, your manhood? Maybe you have masochistic tendencies?"

He sighed heavily, thinking back on it all. A momentary gust of northern air scattered some leaves that had bunched along the curbside. "No, let's not camouflage something much more basic behind a smoke screen of Freudian complexity. 'Love' was a much simpler thing in those more hormonal, insatiable days. Back then, I was in 'love' when any woman who was not autistic could make blood rush to my member. If she would let me have her, I was 'madly in love'."

"How primal," she snorted, "how close to nature."

"My love for this girl was premised primarily upon the sight of her perfectly formed, silver dollar, blood red nipples. The thought of not fondling them again broke me up."

"Well, you still have your imagination."

"Bah!" Sam spit it out impulsively. "How little that is."

With the help of the quiet street and the darkened night, they took refuge in their own thoughts. Edie wondered if the loss of the kind of sexual innocence just described by Sam was the big mistake of her life – or even the big mistake of humanity. Why couldn't she pull the trigger? What more did she have to know? Why keep walking, why, why? But it was impossible, beyond her control – she still didn't feel it.

They game went on.

Chapter 31

Under God

*S*am could not help but think of that frustrated love affair so long ago. Once again, he had to laugh lightly to himself.

"C'mon Sam," Edie broke into his thoughts, slightly annoyed, "people who habitually laugh for no reason can have their sanity brought into question."

"Sorry, I make no claims with regard to my sanity."

"One of the things I demand from people is an explanation for any outbursts of laughter. It makes me feel more relevant."

Her companion continued laughing lightly as he shook his head in disbelief. "You know, I can't even remember her name anymore." He continued shaking his head.

"Who – the latent lesbian in love with Jesus?" Edie could imagine a great song for the Statler Brothers lurking amidst that description.

"I can't even remember her name." It amazed him. He tried to remember. His attempts were interrupted by a barbarian couple on mopeds, rushing by, horns honking, headed for the downtown scene. He kept trying, in spite of the noise. "Nope," he was speaking mainly to himself, "it's gone."

"But you have no trouble remembering her nipples, right?"

"Absolutely none. I can still see them."

Now they both laughed and shook their heads. Edie thought what pathetic creatures human beings really were. We were just smart enough to almost be right, just smart enough to outsmart ourselves at every turn; to pollute the air with fantastic automobiles, to poison ourselves with things to make our food stay fresh, to destroy important ecosystems with spectacular recreational projects, and, perhaps worst of all, the use of our intelligence to invent killing machines that could rival the bubonic plague. At this point in the evolution of the species, our intelligence was more a danger than a solution. Would we make it through these mangy days of Gillette Gods unscathed? The jury was still out.

Edie was so immersed in these thoughts she didn't realize Sam had been talking. "– sent me a copy of the Bible."

"Huh?"

"I was saying that this girl, after she left town in pursuit of her Man –"

"You mean J.C.?"

"Right. She actually sent me a copy of the Bible."

"Just to show she cared."

"I guess – but trading those nipples for such spirituality was something like trading Michael Jordan for my father's 2 hand set shot."

"For you."

Sam felt his sneaker sink into something soft and dangerous. He immediately stopped walking. "Oh shit." He examined the bottom of his foot and was relieved to find he had sunk into a ripe sapodilla. He looked up and saw they were passing under a big tree laden with this exotic fruit.

There were hundreds of "dillies" littering the yard under the tree. A few of them had dropped onto the sidewalk, which had been cracked and raised by the thrust of the old tree's roots. The sweet aroma of fermenting fruit permeated the air. He remembered being in the Lesser Antilles, on the island of Antigua at the height of their mango season. The whole island, an island it took 45 minutes to cross in a car, was luxuriating in the sweet smell of mango. It was almost erotic. "Thank God," he said, as he wiped his shoe on the curb's edge.

"I thought you preferred nipples to God?"

"Smart ass."

"Did you read the Bible?"

Sam continued wiping his shoe. "I read enough to know my heathen status would remain intact." The bottom of his sneaker now satisfied him. He assumed a normal posture as he explained to her. "Look, I respect a person with genuine feelings for God, or Jesus, or Moses, or Muhammad, or Pee Wee Herman, or whatever. The human mind is incredibly creative with regard to these metaphysical creations. If this is the code they need to live by; if this is how they have to answer life's mysteries; if this is their concept of conscience – fine. The fact that someone actually believes in something other than their next new car, is worthy of respect. All I ask is that you don't try to dictate it to others. The transfer of spiritual beliefs into the public discourse is not acceptable. There is a time and place for persuasion, for trying to preach the wisdom of your own particular brand of spiritual dogma, but please, no obligatory stuff! It has no place in the way we govern each other, in the way we manage or defend the wealth of the nation. There simply isn't enough rational data to make any of this mandatory for the whole community; to have it introduced into the public sphere." He stopped and took a deep breath, exhaling like a marathon runner who had just crossed the finish line. "Maybe I'll rot in Hell; maybe they are right and I am wrong; maybe the mountain came to Muhammad; maybe I should only touch one woman, under God, with liberty and justice for all – I'm not claiming I've been to the Mountain. But I defy anyone to show me how all these Gods and Holy Books have given us a more harmonious, secure, fulfilling existence. I think we'd be a hell of a lot better off worrying about each other and not about God." Sam turned away and stared down at the cracked sidewalk. Had he thrown to close to the batter's head? "Sometimes I get a little carried away."

"Don't worry Sam; there are no flies around here."

He thought of taking her hand. Wouldn't any gorilla worth a shit do just that, or even more? Jesus, how could that be such a big decision? He lightly cupped her elbow and gently pointed her down the street. "C'mon, I'll tell you what I found out in the Bible." There was no resistance. On they went.

Chapter 32

A Fatal Error

"So there I was," he spoke as they walked, "in the name of intellectual objectivity –" He stopped walking and furled his brow in thought. "Maybe that really wasn't it."

"Could it be," said Edie, trying to help, "that you still thought you could get her back?"

"Yes, I think I was reading the Bible to please her." He mulled it over. "I somehow thought this really wasn't happening, that it was just a whim, that my taking her seriously would please her." They were now approaching a frangipani tree whose pale yellow flowers had just come out, perhaps within the last day or two. Some of the flowers had already fallen to the ground, probably when the north wind had blown through. Sam picked one up and smelled its barely perceptible aroma. It had a fresh, sweet smell, somewhat reminiscent of cinnamon. His attitude suddenly changed. He laughed briefly and spoke again, this time with an absence of angst. "I never saw or heard from her again, but I did do some Bible reading."

"Obviously," said Edie, as she bent down to grab a fallen frangipani flower, "it hasn't made you a church go-er on Sunday." She deeply inhaled the delicate aroma.

"Hardly," he grunted. "I had a higher opinion of Jesus before I read the Bible."

She continued smelling the flower, eyes closed, blissfully experiencing the natural splendor. "If the Son of

God's father is responsible for this, I'm on board."

"If you could convince me of that, I'd be on board too." They marched on as Sam began to explain. "But reading the Bible certainly didn't convince me of anything. I found out that J.C. may have had a gall bladder for a brain. Not only that, he may have inherited this condition from his father, the **Big Guy**."

Edie laughed. "The **Big Guy**," she said, with a mocking masculine voice.

Sam smiled and went on. "First He goes and invents the planet with the trees and flowers and oceans and insects and birds and scaly, slimy creatures of all kinds. Frangipanis too; a great trick, it can't be denied. But He saves the best for last and creates His most fantastic wonder of all, namely us, in His own likeness too!" Sam stops and laughs.

"There you go again, laughing out of context."

"I was just thinking that if all this is true, God must look like Michael Jordan."

"I don't think the Southern Baptists would go for that."

"Or just about all of white Christendom."

"For sure." She paused for a moment. "They think he looks like Charlton Heston."

Now they both laughed. "In any event," Sam continued, "God sits back and contemplates His work, feeling pretty good about it. At this point he is undecided as to whether He should also invent television –"

"I suppose," intervened Edie, "this is the Samuelian version of the Bible."

"I should hope so. It is the most reliable account of these matters I have ever come across." Edie rolls her eyes, sarcastically nods, and decides to put one of the frangipani flowers carefully in her waist purse. The northern air gently sends forth a touch of cool air. Edie's actions arouse Sam's curiosity. "What are you going to do with that?"

"Oh – I might try to paint it."

"So you're an artist?"

She shrugged. "Something like that."

He didn't press it. "Where were we?"

"God was inventing television."

"Oh yeah – no. He was trying to decide if He should do it or not, but He is feeling so smug about us, the ones in His own likeness, He decides to let us do it for ourselves. He is enamored of us because we are Him."

"Now," Sam continues, "the years and decades and centuries go by and before you know it, God's favorite most fantastic invention is turning out to be an unruly gang of slovenly, drunken fornicators. Especially the latter! Damned if He didn't get carried away with that penis-vagina thing. What a great idea. Too good! Nobody wanted to do anything else and they hadn't even invented TV yet. How's it look when your best trick can't even do that?"

Edie shook her head. "Bad P.R., no doubt about it."

"So God was getting a little pissed because His most fantastic creation was paying more attention to this, that and especially the slippery-slidey thing, and not enough to Him."

"I think I know what's wrong," said Edie, cutting in. "It's like a catch 22; God invented us in His own likeness, which means we inherited His well developed ego. Our ego and His ego are constantly challenging each other."

"Edie," said an exasperated Sam, "will you let me

finish?"

"You see," she said, pointing an accusatory finger his way, "you've got his ego." They laughed again. "But go ahead anyway."

"So God decides to send His only Son down there to see if He could grab the attention of the forefathers of our current crop of Jerry Springer fans."

"Jerry Springer," said our lady solemnly, "Sodom and Gomorrah, global economy style."

"Right. God was really embarrassed that His best invention, the ones who were supposed to be like Him, had turned out to be a mob of hollow headed clods. So here comes Jesus to save the day. But He turns out to be an incompetent chip off the Old Block. He comes on like some know it all magician, telling everyone he's where it's at, spouting riddles and homily chicken soup catch phrases, and He puts most everyone uptight. In spite of his bag of flashy tricks – walking on water and all that – J.C. gets Himself pinned to a post and the Big Guy –"

"The **Big Guy**," interrupted Edie, using her masculine voice.

Sam burst out laughing. He was now thoroughly bewitched by this woman. Failure would be a serious blow. It was scary.

When he composed himself, he went on. "That's right, the Big Guy. He's still competing with Jerry Springer and Larry Flynt for adepts. That's a pretty sorry track record after all these centuries, don't you think?"

"Gosh Sam, you sound like some kind of spin master for the opposition."

The cutting sound of a siren began making inroads in

their consciousness. It soon became evident it was coming their way. As it drew closer, they braced for its arrival in much the same way a cornerback might prepare for the arrival of a fullback in the open field. They tensed their bodies and covered their ears. The ambulance sped by at a blinding speed, lights flashing, motor roaring, something was amuck in paradise.

As it raced off towards the downtown area, they began to slowly uncoil and relax. Edie spoke first. "I guess the anti-Christ is loose in some barroom brawl, eh?"

"Could be." They continued walking. Edie's spin master comment was not sitting well with our man. He felt the need to reply. "Hey Edie, I'm not into 'spin'. Perhaps one of the fatal errors of my life was to join the army of truth seekers. Being that 'hype' and 'spin' have become the foundation of western society, this puts me in a perpetual state of opposition. It's become a very difficult row to hoe."

"Something like what Jesus was doing, wouldn't you say?"

Sam pondered the cogent remark. In a way, that's what Jesus stood for. He was humanity's conscience. He stood in opposition to all the self-serving spin masters since the dawn of time. He was the universal loser vainly trying to rectify the hopeless imperfections of an imperfect world. Not only couldn't he defeat the spin masters, he had been absorbed by them, out maneuvered by them, co-opted by them. "Yeah," he said ironically, "and look what it got him."

Chapter 33

Fish Stories

They were now less than 3 blocks from Jackson Street, the main commercial artery of downtown South Isle. The noise and bluster of the global economy in the form of tourism could already be felt. Up ahead, an endless stream of traffic tediously navigated Jackson Street in impatient stutter steps of 50 to 100 yards. An occasional motorcycle roar, along with the more constant backdrop of horns and idling motors, punctuated the night air. A steady mass of pedestrian flow flanked the glacier-like movement of the vehicular intensity. The distant thump of pop music leaked unconsciously into the atmosphere and the street itself was lit like an indoor arena.

"There is one thing you said," Edie spoke as they walked towards this hive of obligatory fun, "that I still want to ask you about."

"Shoot."

"You said you had a higher opinion of Jesus before you read the Bible. That seems a bit peculiar to me."

They were approaching the old public library. Now more than 125 years old, it had a kind of grace that never went out of style. Its tile roof was reminiscent of colonial Spain, but the tiles, in another display of cultural fusion, were the dark grey of a more Anglo slate material. They covered a low lying, rambling structure with pale pink walls surrounded by well-kept grounds. It was a graceful edifice set into its environment in much the same way a lithe gazelle belonged on the African plains. It was a beloved place.

"I'd be glad to explain," he said, "but I'd have to do it before we go up into that." He nodded towards the mindless, carefree bustle up ahead. "Why don't we sit here on the library steps? I've always loved this place."

They sat down in the dim light provided by the antique lamps of the building's entrance. From here, the turmoil of Jackson Street was still just a minor provocation. The sweet smell of night blooming jasmine wafted through the air. Being that there were some "gay" guesthouses in the area, an occasional group of men passed by in pursuit of the night's revelry.

"It's true," he started, "some of the things I read in the Bible actually made Jesus look – silly – or dumb."

"Like what?"

"Well –" he thoughtfully put a finger over his mouth and tried to conjure it up all over again. "Oh yeah – listen to this one. One day J.C. was stirring things up by Lake Genneserat. The usual mob of turdlings were groveling around, waiting for Him to lay some kind of flashy trick on them –"

"Once again," she couldn't help herself, "we are using the Samuelian version of the Bible, correct?"

"Can you think of a more reliable source?" Edie shrugged and blew out her horse snort, unwilling to commit to anything more than that. But Sam would have none of it. "I don't think so." She said nothing. "Anyway, Jesus, probably feeling a bit woozy from the close pressing crowd of scuzballs gathered around Him, asked some nearby fishermen if they could carry Him a bit out from shore. Being that J.C. was a VIP in this neck of the desert, his request was eagerly granted and He gave His sermon buffered from the mangy gathering by a short expanse of water."

"J.C. preached a nice set and figured he'd top it all off with a hot shit miracle, because, let the truth be known, this is what His fans were really waiting for. Noticing the fishermen had caught no fish that day, J.C calmly told the boys to put out a bit further and drop their nets. This set off a buzz amongst the fleabags on shore, many of whom had been dozing dreamily during the sermon. 'This is it. He's gonna do something'. The mob pressed closer to the shoreline in anticipation of the day's great event. Sure enough, faster than you could say Osama Bin Laden –"

Edie threw her head back and laughed without affectation. "I have to admit, this is the best version of the Bible I've ever heard."

"Quit interrupting." Sam had to laugh as well. "So there He was, and before anyone had time to think about it, the fish were swarming the nets in a volcanic eruption of twitching gills and spastic desperation. Nobody had ever seen so many fish before in this lake. Unbelievable!"

Edie didn't get it. "So? – That sounds pretty good to me."

"Ah hah, but here comes the good part – J.C. reminds me of a pitcher who can throw 100 mph but never learns how to pitch. He's like the anti-El Duque. He's flashy, he catches your attention, but he doesn't pan out in the end."

"Look, Sam, He just caught all this fish. There were no

fish before. Fish!"

"But that's not how the story ends. The fish come so fast and furious that the nets began to break. J.C. was probably trying to remember the antidote for the old-fish-in-the-net-trick as the boat sunk under all that fish weight." Edie grunted internally as she mulled the story over. "Does that sound like something to brag about?"

"Do you think the fishermen had insurance?"

Our theologian, wrapped in his own thoughts, did not hear Edie's joke. He gazed blindly into the dimly lit Old Barrio landscape. "It's a miracle," he mumbled.

"A miracle?"

"I can still remember the Biblical citation. Luke 5: 4-7. You can look it up."

Chapter 34

Richard Burton and Rex Harrison

A group of homosexuals passed by the library steps, chattering merrily, flirting amongst themselves, already into their partying mode. It was easy to see how the word "gay" had become associated with this sub-culture. One of them, with an overdose of femininity, greeted them and asked, "Well now, what are you two up to?"

Sam smiled and shook his head. "We're still trying to figure it out."

"Well," he moved a bit like Marilyn Monroe, all pouting lips and erotic suggestion, away from the protocol of his job or the straight world in general, "I hope it all works out, if you know what I mean."

Sam knew what he meant.

"Ta, ta." The merry band moved on towards Jackson Street, trailing a palpable scent of perfume and aftershave.

They sat silently for awhile, watching the boys flitter away into the night. "What a world," said Sam, smiling ironically.

"Some people," said Edie, "think Jesus was a homosexual."

"Not a totally implausible idea. The Apostles seemed to have been a rather tight knit group – don't you think?"

Edie leaned back and took in the full bouquet of the jasmine perfume all around her. It was a dense aroma, something that could almost be worn like clothing. She breathed deeply and straightened up. "Sometimes I wonder what goes on at the Vatican. Imagine all those Cardinals glittering in jewels and satin robes, living under one roof in a spectacular baroque palace – Hey, think about it."

"I'd rather not." They sat for awhile, privately juggling their own thoughts. A light touch of northern air wafted down from Canada. Edie pulled Sam's jacket a bit more tightly around herself.

Edie was not a believer, but she had been brought up in a Catholic environment and felt, much to her surprise, somewhat uncomfortable with Sam's disdain. "But Sam," she interjected uneasily, "maybe he wasn't the brightest guy in the world, but Jesus did seem to identify with the common man."

"That's what I always thought, until I read the Bible." Our lady seemed to have touched a raw nerve. Sam sat up and spoke with more purpose. "Sometimes he seemed like a social climber or power freak – at times he reminded me of an ambitious politician."

"Harsh words Sam."

He relaxed and lay back on the steps once again. He was trying to remember one particular episode that had always stayed with him. "You're right, he supposedly represented the common man; power to the people, the meek shall inherit the Wall Street Journal, stuff like that. In truth, he probably did consider these people to be his constituents but he really didn't know how to serve their interests – though he was very good at keeping them enthralled with flashy tricks."

"Documentation Sam."

"Well, as I remember –" he pressed his lips tightly,

trying to visualize the story he was trying to conjure up, "J.C. was cruising around the desert one day when He was besieged by a certain Roman centurion whose favorite slave had fallen seriously ill. Now this Roman soldier was anything but poor or humble, which he vividly pointed out to our dimwitted miracle maker. In no uncertain terms he explained how powerful he was, how he could tell a man to shit chicken croquettes and he'd have to do it –

"Now that's what I call real power," said Edie, laughing lustily.

"You bet. But now he stood before J.C. pleading for His help because he'd heard He could pull off that kind of stuff, namely, cure his slave, who he needed to wash his underwear."

"Men of great power," said Edie, "never clean underwear."

"If the truth must be known –"

She cut in. "One of the fatal mistakes of your life, right Sam?"

"It's important for the truth to be recorded somewhere, even if it's just for the sake of future archeologists."

"Proceed Sam, if only for posterity."

"Thank you," he said sarcastically as he returned to his story. "In any event, this soldier was really no more than a tin horn gladiator stuck out there in the colonies, far from the bright lights of Rome, but to good old J.C. he came on like Richard Burton and Rex Harrison all rolled into one. Perhaps hoping to get free seats to the next big show at the Coliseum, He cured the slave, who was immediately sent to the laundry room. The fact that this centurion had probably raped and pillaged his way around the world – not to mention the idea of slavery – didn't seem to bother the Son of God. I remember thinking when I first read this stuff –"

"Can you remember the Biblical citation for this one?"

Once again, he tightened his lips and skewered his face in thought. He stared blankly at 2 beautifully restored Victorian homes standing side by side across the street. "I remember thinking," he repeated, "that J.C. seemed more like a lobbyist than a populist when I read that." He stared down at the ground as he continued thinking. "I almost have it –" He was enthralled in concentration. "Luke 7: 6-10."

Chapter 35

This Thing "God"

"It's amazing how you can still remember the citations." Sam could only shake his head. It had been so long ago. What an amazing data bank the human mind was – but it wasn't just that. Feelings and circumstance, things psychological and emotional; they all played a role. The brain was not just an efficient computer that spit up information on cue. The fact that he was here with this desirable woman, trying to deal with his most basic desires; the fact that his reading the Bible was spurred on by a similar need so many years ago, had probably activated his mind and helped trigger his memory. But he still couldn't think of that girl's name.

"Was it Katherine – or Kathy? She kind of looked like a Katherine."

Edie was off somewhere in her own thoughts. "When I think about it – I can remember a similar Bible story that put 'the first shall be last' doctrine in doubt for me."

Sam realized she had not been listening to him. "Were you ever much of a believer?" He anxiously wondered if she still might have some religious "faith."

"Not really. I took the cure at an early age."

"The cure?"

"I went to Catholic schools."

They both laughed. "That's cured a lot of people, hasn't it?"

"It's to religion what the Salk vaccine is to polio." She paused for a moment, trying to remember something from her religious education. "But I can vaguely remember one story –" Now it was her turn to try and conjure up something from her brush with the Bible. "I was just a little girl – but wasn't there an anecdote where Jesus shows up in a poor home with his filthy feet –"

"I know the one you mean," Sam blurted out, as if he were in class and wanted to impress the teacher. "J.C. was –"

"No, no," she broke in, "let me try and remember." She sat up on the steps and scanned the star lit sky. She spoke to the stars. "There was a woman in this wretched hut who had beautiful long hair. It was decided they would wipe off Jesus' feet with her hair, using a very expensive ointment that was almost gone." She continued staring into the sky, trying to recall it all.

"You're getting to the good part," said Sam, "do you want some help?"

"Someone suggested that the ointment was very good stuff and they had very little left – and maybe it would be better to let the poor people use it instead of wiping off Jesus' feet. But, as I remember, J.C. vetoed the idea, saying there'd always be plenty of poor people around, while anointing Him was a once in a lifetime opportunity." She sat up and looked at Sam. She shrugged. "Something like that."

"You got it. Those events come from John12 –" He tried to remember the exact citation. "I can't remember exactly, but John12 is where it comes from."

"Mind you Sam, this was long before I had any feel for

144

Feminism or women's issues, or who or what I wanted to be. But even as a little girl, I felt something here that I didn't like."

"You mean, as a woman?"

"Yes, something degrading or – I don't know – not quite right. I remember thinking to myself, 'darn, he's not going to use my hair for that'."

Another insolent group of moped barbarians sped past the library steps. Adding to the tinny noise of their whining motors was the usual chorus of honking horns and adolescent shouting. The drivers weaved and dodged in and out, almost dangerously. Sam wondered what turned a person into an instant child upon mounting a moped. Being that the wind had almost died, they left the predictable trail of petroleum perfume hanging in the air. He far preferred the homosexual aftershave to this piggy display of the fossil fuel habit.

The clatter of the intrusion retreated into the night. Sam spoke into the reborn silence. "I've always had trouble with this thing 'God'."

Edie shrugged impatiently and ran her fingers through her short blond hair. She almost seemed annoyed, as she did when depressed people had entered the conversation. "So does everyone else," she said with attitude, "even those who say they believe in God. God has simply become part of the baggage of our culture, something we all inherit mindlessly when we are born. The mainstream concept of God is such a simple minded thing that it needs the full onslaught of a 21st Century sound machine, pounding it into our brains, just to keep it afloat. For most people, God is something they turn to when they need help. For most people, God does absolutely nothing to shape their behavior. Most people are far more influenced by the economic system they live under and the incessant commercial messages they hear than by anything they listen to in church or about God. I'm not saying there is or isn't a God – but the one set forth by our culture –" she stopped and let loose her derisive horse snort, "nobody really trusts it, no matter what the pledge of allegiance says."

Sam had taken in this philosophical outburst in awe struck devotion. What a woman, he thought to himself. He impulsively leaned forward and tried to kiss her on the lips. She turned her head slightly, allowing the amorous impact to fall Platonically on her cheek. He slumped his shoulders and turned away, sighing heavily.

Edie touched him on the arm and made him look at her. "Don't be upset Sam. It's my problem as much as yours. This game is still in progress. It ain't over 'til it's over." He turned away, secretly amused that she had used the old Yogi Berra quote. But it did not change his melancholy mood. He stared into the empty street. The familiar brooding quality once again clamped down on his face. Another group of merry homosexuals approached from down the street. They were happy. They were ready to enjoy. Sam envied their uncluttered ability to simply have fun. "C'mon Sam, let's go downtown."

Part 2

Chapter 1

Jersey City

*I*t was the height of the tourist season. To say that Jackson Street was crowded did not do justice to this familiar cliché of the world on vacation. The mobs of people cruising up and down the street could better be described as a flood tide of humanity. Over the years, as South Isle solidified itself as a "tourist destination resort," Sam had become convinced that with the right marketing approach, there was not a place on the face of the Earth that could not be made to attract tourists. Come to Jersey City, he thought to himself, see the historic port, the bar where Frank Sinatra first sang, the world famous Mafia Museum, the best view of New York harbor, take the tour, get a tee shirt, just minutes from downtown New York. Kevin Costner's movie with the baseball field had it all wrong; "build it and they will come" should really be "promote it and they will come." Amen.

Being that the island was 150 miles from the mainland, it had developed in its own isolation. Many people who ended up here were a rather offbeat agglomeration of cultural misfits and refugees. Even the Lenos, who spoke with an accent that could not be heard anywhere else, had renegade qualities, their original ancestors having been Tories who'd escaped to the Bahamas during the American Revolution and later made their way to South Isle. This place always had a Wild West, anything goes kind of reputation, a partying town where you could come down and do as you please. It was the kind of place where you could get silly, where you could be a jerk for awhile before returning to the post you held down as a solid citizen. Regardless of the economic metamorphosis of the moment, down through South Isle's almost 2 centuries of existence, this ask no questions, do your own thing attitude had always been at the core of the island's personality.

But the voracious global economy, like some insatiable Pac Man gobbling everything in its path, had managed to coerce this free spirit for its own designs. The island was now just a caricature of itself, something used to sell and market to the vacationing masses. South Isle had been dragged into the "real world" –albeit reluctantly, like a stubborn mule kicking and snorting in protest –but in the end it had succumbed to the tyrannical dictates of a money-driven world.

This attitude was reflected in the economic make up of Jackson Street. For the 10 blocks that covered its most commercial part, there were multiple bars on every block, bars that catered to every taste: gay bars, "yee ha" bars with live rock bands, elegant watering holes with piano bars, sports bars with TV's looking down from all angles, bars for "women," "world famous" bars whose tee shirts and logos were known outside of South Isle, titty bars for the more horny, bars that hearkened back to the hippy days with folk singers and acoustic guys singing their own creations or doing requests of all kinds. And restaurants! From the greasy practicality of fast food, donut shops, pizza parlors, ice cream stands, hot dogs and burgers, to truly elegant dining with fresh filets of fish smothered in sauces and garnishes with exotic foreign names, all pretension and over-priced atmosphere with Chevalier-like waiters constantly filling your water glass and changing your fork.

And, of course, shopping. In a society based primarily on buying, selling, and the possession of "stuff," "shopping" had become one of the focal points of a successful vacation. Sam had never understood why this mundane activity, which could be done just as well at home, had become such an integral part of the generic vacation. Ironically, before the island had become such a mainstream "tourist destination," there had been an interesting conjunction of off beat shops and emporiums that provided a unique commercial experience. These small businesses represented the singular style and attitude of what was once an out of the way place: wonderful little shops where local artisans and craftsmen displayed their work, clothing stores that reflected the tropical, laid back personality of the island, businesses that upheld the best kind of "Jeffersonian," little man entrepreneurship.

With the advent of Wall Street tourism, all this had changed. The masses and the money they brought with them had raised the ante and driven the little man out. "Shopping" along Jackson Street had disintegrated into a predictable medley of well-known outlets like Coach, Panama Jack, Banana Republic and such. But even more disturbing was the invasion of the tee shirt shops, all offering the same merchandise in a crass world of jaundiced neon light, loud pop music and shifty, usurious salesmanship. Underneath the well-honed subterfuge of individual ownership, all these shops were controlled by a nebulous world of Middle East racketeers, using this tee shirt scam for their own clandestine reasons, probably to launder the vast sums of money they had made in some underworld of illegality. These people had shown up unexpectedly, with gigantic bankrolls they used to buy up the property at over the market prices. They then bullied the previous renters out with exorbitant rental hikes, leaving the uninspiring commercial spectacle already alluded to. This had become the face of "tourism," not just in South Isle, but in many places where this vast industry had now become its livelihood.

In closing this descriptive parenthesis, it is not superfluous to note that this town – like just about every other place deemed "successful" by status quo definition – was now strangling itself in automobiles.

As Sam and Edie anonymously walked the strip, invisibly blending in with the vacationing hordes, they felt an almost pleasant kind of alienation, content in knowing they were "outsiders" here, that they were not true consumers of the vacation hustle.

Our couple stopped on one of the busiest corners in this desperate whirlwind of humans seeking to amuse themselves. The whole neon lit symphony of blaring music, revving engines, honking horns and the simple presence of so many people in such little space, converged in a thunderous rip tide of spam-like noise. The herd moved implacably, like some huge, amorphous blob of mercury. Most of them were underdressed in the brisk night air, shivering in shorts, tee shirts and halter-tops. It was as if they were in a state of denial – this was the tropics, goddamit – refusing to believe it was a bit too cool for such clothing.

This was assembly line tourism in all its glory and decadence.

As Sam scanned this vast plain of tourist impalas in their ritual migrations, he began thinking out loud. "Yes, we know who you are, when you're coming, how much you'll spend, what you want to eat, how much liquor you'll consume, when you will leave, if you'll come back, how you got here. We've done the research. We know if you have hemorrhoids, how many of you will get diarrhea, who'll bring the kids, where you come from, where you work, how much you earn, how much you owe, what credit cards you have, how many of you we will have to throw in jail or treat at the emergency room. There's no mystery here, no romance, no adventure, nothing poetic. Here you are, here's your Fat Tuesday, your Hard Rock, your tee shirt shop. You'll feel right at home here. Next year you can go to the same place in a different location. Here –"

They stood awhile longer on the bustling street corner. The night's activity swirled around them in a senseless haze, as if they were in focus and everything else was slightly blurred – or was it the other way around? Edie snapped out of it first. In an effort to be clearly understood, she spoke directly into Sam's ear. "You know what's the saddest part of all this?" He turned and looked at her. "None of this serves any enlightening purpose. It's mindless, pre-packaged, artificially flavored. It's like going away from home without ever leaving your house. It doesn't broaden your horizons."

Sam could only shrug and nod in agreement. "You know, I hope they never turn Jersey City into a tourist trap."

Edie seemed confused. "Is there something I missed?"

He smiled, shook his head and looked directly into her beautiful face. "No. I think you have a complete understanding of the situation."

Chapter 2

Dr. Phil

*E*die and Sam entered a bar that had remained remarkably consistent down through the years, one that still held the vague atmosphere of the 60's and 70's. Faceless forms sifted anonymously through the barely visible murk, clinging to walls or corners or seated at the bar. There were also a series of tables looking out on Jackson Street, whose occupants could watch the mass migration at their leisure as they worked on their beverages. Candlelight encased in glass containers provided a discrete illumination for the night's participants, be they consummated lovers, uncertain couples a la Sam and Edie, or simply unattached men and women, in groups or alone, in search of the erotic reward that is truly the engine of human motivation.

An attractive girl, with lustrous, long black hair tamed somewhat by an Indian style headband, competently attacked Clapton's "I Shot the Sheriff" to the general indifference of the restless clientele. She was accompanied on guitar by a man whose wild red hair and bushy mustache gave him a look reminiscent of Buffalo Bill Cody. A rhythm machine filled out the band, faithfully keeping the beat with mechanical precision.

On the opposite side of the room, separated by the U-shaped bar from the slightly raised stage where the musicians toiled without glory, were 2 pool tables. Nicotine smoke rose densely through the stark neon glare above the less than lush billiard surface. The mood was one of darkened anarchy, allowing the nebulous humanoids to seek their destinies without being self-conscious. Nothing anyone did in here was anyone's business. A woman could let herself be picked up, or a man could get shot down without accountability. This was the human burlesque in all its glory.

As the two of them elbowed up to the bar, Sam could not help but think how much time he had logged in places like this, usually unsuccessfully, usually with a great sense of defeat and anxiety that hid behind a mask of youthful mirth and confidence.

"Question Edie."

Our fair damsel was busy blinking her eyes, trying to deal with the irritation caused by the noisy, stuffy, smoke filled environment. She had not heard Sam's request.

"Edie!"

"What?" She was now rubbing her eyes with her knuckles.

"Why is it that men and women are sent off to dicker with each other in places like this?"

She stopped rubbing but continued blinking until some kind of focus returned. She scanned the crowded room, taking in this familiar scene with all her senses. The music was loud but tasty, with Pocahontas now sweetly crooning a decent rendition of **groovin', on a Sunday afternoon** –Unfortunately, it was no more than a vestigial after thought in the mixed din which permeated the place –the endless conversation, the crisp smack of billiard balls, the bar maid ringing her tip bell, the traffic and noise drifting in from the street and the general loutishness associated with such venues. She had to speak loudly just to be heard.

"Good question Sam." She rubbed her eyes a bit more and continued scanning the room. "I suppose people in search of their next orgasm need such uproar in order to succeed. They need to get out of themselves, to leave the truth or reality behind. The alcohol, the noise, the hazy ambiguity – in truth, I used to need it too. I needed to not be thinking, to be vulnerable –" She paused and glanced up at the singer. **Groovin'** – Turning back to Sam she went on. "Funny, but now it's just the opposite; I must be completely lucid, thoroughly in control." She rubbed the space between her eyes. An embarrassed smile barely appeared on her lips. Sighing deeply, she added, "Who the hell am I, Dr. Phil?"

Sam laughed. He thought back on his predictable lack of success in places like this. Although he had somehow blundered into his fair share of amorous fulfillment, he could hardly remember ever having "scored" in this kind of environment. He had always been way too honest with himself, way too conscious of his acts to be able to come out of character in search of a blowjob. It wasn't a question of guilt – God knows, as mentioned before in this tale, just don't be retarded, have the right accessories, let's go. But he could never pull that off; he was always clumsy enough to let the woman know he cared for nothing more than the orgasm she could provide – or at least she could feel it. He'd suffered for this unavoidable sincerity. The truth was always the most difficult road to navigate.

"I think for people like you or I Edie – or perhaps I

should only speak for myself – these places now serve virtually no purpose. I am much too honest with myself, much too imprisoned in who I am and what I expect from others. I'm not against casual encounters, but it must be something that both sides are perfectly agreed upon, something that doesn't come along all that often. It's something I cannot chase after anymore. I think I am doomed to something more serious from here on out."

Edie shuddered slightly as she eyed the room. "God Sam, we're beginning to sound downright scary."

The barmaid arrived with a smile and asked what they wanted. They looked at each other and didn't have to speak. Sam left a dollar on the bar as they turned and headed for the door. The doorman-bouncer eyed Edie as she approached, trying to make some kind of eye contact. No dice. Sam led the way onto the street. They merged into the impala herd. The odyssey continued.

"Woo!" said Sam, wiping a few pearls of sweat from his brow.

Chapter 3

Nostalgia

*O*ur duo took their insignificant places in the herd's ranks. They let its primordial course carry them along. By now, the original feeling of pleasant alienation had disappeared. This was something they were all too familiar with and the novelty of actually taking part in it had lost its luster. This is not where they belonged. It was no longer an exercise in a local's amused perusal of the tourists. They needed to get out.

"C'mon," said Sam, "follow me."

Edie fell in behind him as they picked up the pace. They were no longer drifting with all the other impalas, but dodging and sifting their way out of the maze. When they had reached the end of Jackson Street, they turned to the left and followed the street which bordered the cruise ship port on the northwest extremity of the island. To their right, looming over the city like something from a Japanese monster movie, was the awesome bulk of a dazzling white cruise ship. Its superstructure was brightly festooned with thousands of lights. The barely perceived tinkle of calypso music drifted out from the dock it was tied to.

One of the more remarkable aspects of a once charming place's descent into the "tourist trap" label, is how much of it can be attributed to one man. This one man's ability to take over a place's personality and shape it to his own needs has little to do with intelligence, good taste, vision or creativity. It has almost nothing to do with anything more than ambition. Some might prefer to call it "greed," but for those of us who have seen this behavior in close quarters, such a word seems too simple a concept. Quite early in the game, the entrepreneur has amassed enough of a fortune to make the idea of making more money superfluous. What soon takes over is an irrational necessity to propagate a "persona" or self-image. This Chamber-of-Commerce-hero identity must be nourished in ever increasing amounts, like a compulsive eater who can't stop gorging himself on strawberry shortcake. Once this kind of ambition finds an economic vacuum to operate in, the results can be devastating.

South Isle's "one man" was a fair haired Leno named Tom Lento, a forever smiling Rotary Club kind of guy whose life consisted of nothing more than nursing his garden of forever swelling business interests. Tom Lento wanted to grow the biggest business tomato South Isle had ever seen.

Sam and Edie had now entered the heart of the Lento Empire.

Ironically, although this area was the hub of the downtown tourist environment, this block or two in close proximity to the cruise port was the peaceful eye of the storm raging all around it – but only at night. During the day, it was the primary staging ground for the guided tours – Lento owned tours – that carried thousands of people around in an endless procession of slow moving surrey covered "trains" or Frisco-like "trolleys." Perhaps more than any other thing on the island, this eternal intrusion of these "Wally World" tours, with their incessant, banal, amplified chatter; with their dumb founded clientele staring cow-like at the scenery, gave South Isle the undesired tourist trap label it now deserved. For many residents, it was the most hated institution on the island, the most representative example of what could not be turned back anymore.

But at night this compact area was a totally different place. The cutesy trolleys and trains were all gone, put neatly to bed in their garages on the neighboring island 5 miles away. The whole series of trinket shops – conveniently owned by Lento – which served the deluge of cruise ship passengers who numbly took the tours; the palm frond, beany bag, parrot head, blown glass, coconut carved, shell painted souvenirs apt for a tropical island, were all locked in recuperative repose in anticipation of the next day's commerce. This area was now a cove of tranquility just off the hard pounding ocean it was sprung from.

Having entered this surprising cove of tranquility, our couple had unconsciously returned to a more leisurely pace. Sam led the way down a narrow alleyway to where the huge "love boat" – Lento was a prime player in the ever growing cruise ship presence – was docked. At this hour, somewhere near the midnight meridian, most of the passengers were snug on the ship. The predictable calypso band mechanically added to the festive mood. The musicians were dressed in colorful tropical shirts with Satchmo-like smiles carved into their weathered black faces. This was their last set and they could soon have a quick drink and head home for a few hours sleep before getting wearily up for their real jobs the next morning. Their music was innocuous, inoffensive, competent.

Sam led Edie to the last bulkhead on the dock, where the huge rope from the ship's stern kept the mammoth white beast tight to shore. The rope was so thick that Sam could not come close to getting his hand around it.

They sat down on the edge of the dock, a few feet behind the bulkhead. Although they were 30 yards behind the ship's stern, it loomed over them like a gigantic tidal wave poised to roll over on itself. It flew a Norwegian flag, claimed its homeport as Monrovia, Liberia, and was named "Her Royal Majesty." Obviously, thought Sam, some kind of corporate ruse in search of higher profits in the global economy.

"The taxi cab drivers in this town," he remarked, while marveling at the sheer size of the vessel, "have a generic name for all these cruise ships."

"What?"

"'Her Royal Fucking Majesty'"

Edie laughed lightly and grunted. "Perfect."

Off to the left – or the south – were 2 more berths for cruise ships, both currently empty. The docks were not attached and one could not walk from one to the other. Beyond the dim light provided on these docks was the darkness of the ship channel, broken only by the constellation of red and green navigation lights blinking chaotically on their black canvas background. A large congregation of gulls, pelicans and cormorants could be seen on the neighboring dock. Sam had often marveled at these feathered concentrations. They always seemed to be very social gatherings, as if our winged friends were "partying." Even Tom Lento couldn't change that.

"How long have you lived here Edie?"

"Oh, about 22-3 years."

"Amazing how we never really talked before."

162

Edie stared out at the blackness to the west, imagining the mangrove islands that hung precariously on the horizon during the daylight hours. Certainly, much of her time had been taken up by a number of long term relationships she'd had while living here. Being the proper middle class girl she was she didn't make herself available during those stretches of time. She also knew, just from years of casual observation, that Sam had been involved a couple of times as well –and, in truth, from afar he had never really interested her.

"How long have you been here?"

"Wow –" he shook his head, finding it hard to believe. "More than 35 years – it doesn't seem that long." He seemed to lose himself in his own thoughts, as if he were being transported back to a different time and place. He turned around and took in the scene all around him. An unwelcome wave of nostalgia swept over him. This place was his home – there was no more doubt about that – but it wasn't what it used to be. But life's experience had also taught him the perfection sought during one's years of youthful exuberance didn't really exist anywhere. It was an illusion – like truth and justice for all or even true love, though he had to sadly admit he still stubbornly sought them both. At least he had become more realistic in his march into middle age. Everyone had to be somewhere and when he heard the tourists bemoaning their fates on the days they had to return home, he'd decided there was no point in fighting it. But at the current moment in this story, he couldn't help it.

"When you first got here Edie, this was still a pretty genuine place, so I'd guess we share some kinship with regard to our local attitudes. But it was just starting to change. I can still remember a night I spent on this dock –"

Not a Love Story

Chapter 4

Orthodontists

"*I* had come down here one summer night, just to relax. The girl I was living with was working. We'd been with each other for a few years and it was starting to get stale. I needed to get out, to think about things." He stopped and looked all around once again. On either side of the dock a modern skyline of hotels and time-share resorts framed its location. The distant din of the tourist hustle on Jackson Street reminded him of what they had just left behind. "In those days this was a very different place. Can you remember any of that?"

She had a dim image of what it was like when she'd first arrived. "As I remember, this area was like – I don't know – like a real working port area."

"Right."

"But within a year or so it all started to change, so I can't really see it anymore – it was never a solid part of my reality here."

Sam looked slightly to his right in search of what was once known as Oil Island, a low lying chunk of land that used to be covered in pine scrub. The Navy had once had tanks for petroleum storage there. It had recently been sold by the military, no longer being deemed necessary for the defense of the nation. A private developer was now building luxury homes out there. The Navy had never been too zealous in its possession and there was some nice beach property on the side that faced away from the city. Being out there was like being on the far side of the moon. It was a great place to go skinny-dipping with a loved one, or to throw a memorable party – sunsets, pot, beer, food, music – young people at the top of their game, in the springtime of life, as if they owned the world. But the global economy had struck again – or had he just gotten old? The bulk of "Her Royal Fucking Majesty" obliterated a glimpse of the fondly remembered island.

"Your memory is pretty good," Sam went on. "This was a real port area, with repair shops, net shops, shrimp boats, marine supply stores and stuff like that. Small freighters and tankers used to come in here all the time. The night I was just referring to I sat down right here, by this same bulkhead."

"At least that's still here," our lady interjected, peering once again towards the unseen mangrove islands.

"Instead of this gargantuan creature tied up here now, there was a rusty hulled freighter. It was about ¼ the size of this thing and was moored to those bulkheads further down the dock." He indicated with his head as he spoke. "There were three leathery faced black men fishing from the stern of the – I guess 'tramp steamer' would be a good way to describe it. I could barely hear their leisurely chatter but they spoke with that beautiful down island accent most associated with Jamaica. It all spoke of the sea, of sudden Caribbean storms, of Barbados rum and Haitian voodoo, of exotic ports with magnificent tropical backdrops."

Sam stopped and lay down on his back. He gazed into the sky. Only the most obvious constellations were visible, the light from the downtown area having somewhat obstructed the stellar view. "Am I boring you?"

"Don't be silly Sam, there are very few flies out tonight." She lay back as well, peering into the heavens as he spoke.

"As I listened to the relaxed conversation of the crew, with their far off accents – I don't know, there was something magnetic for me. My own life seemed bogged down, trivial. I got up and strolled towards the old freighter, just to see where it was from."

A flock of egrets in their v-shaped traveling formation flew quickly by like a mirage in the sky. The light from the ground reflected off their snow colored forms. Although they were gone in a matter of seconds, it was impossible not to be impressed by these flying ghosts.

"Wow!" said Edie, momentarily dazzled by the aviary display, "what could be more exotic than that?"

Sam continued staring into the sky. His thoughts were still with that night more than 30 years ago. "For me, Edie, that rusty old ship with its third world crew was the most exotic thing I'd ever seen. I got close to the stern and tried to read its homeport, but the letters were all chipped and rusted. I listened awhile to the sweet chant of the sailors' down island English-Patois. I couldn't understand it all, but they seemed to be talking about women, all smiles and laughter. When they lapsed into a silent moment, I could not help but shout up at them; 'hey man, where you from?' 'St. Lucia, mon.' 'Where's that?' 'Down nea' da Grenadines, mon.'

I nodded though I didn't know where any of that was. I went home that night and immediately looked in my atlas."

"Where is it?"

"Uh, you know, down by Trinidad and Martinique and all that."

"I was down to Dominica once. I can't ever remember being in a more beautiful place; crystal clear waters, natural white sand beaches, green mountain peaks, goats and cows roaming around, their bells tinkling. It was third world but very civilized."

Sam inflated his cheeks and blew out heavily in a sad sigh of recognition. Just like that night so long ago, he wished he could be down there right now. He imagined himself in some small hotel with Edie within walking distance of a secluded cove ringed with pearly sand –" I asked them where they had come from. 'Miami, mon.' 'Where are you going?' 'To da' Sponish coast an' den home t' St. Lucia.' 'What are you carrying?' 'Palm oil, mon.' At that moment I'd have given anything to be one of them, to be cruising the Caribbean –"

Edie cut in. "Forget it Sam, we had the misfortune of growing up with shopping malls and orthodontists."

The easily digestible calypso music, dancing lightly in the crisp night air, brought Sam back to reality. He sat up and turned to his right, watching the generic cruise ship passengers straggle back to the ship. Like most of the impalas seen recently on Jackson Street, they were under dressed in shorts and tropical shirts. Unlike the calypso band musicians, they had no clothing under their shirts. Almost all of them were pecking away on their tweety-facebook devices, letting everyone know what a great time they were having. Some were taking pictures with the same devices. He shook his head and sighed heavily once again.

Edie continued on her back, staring into the sky.

"What's wrong Sam?" She could feel his edginess.

He lay down on his back again and stared at the Big Dipper. Where was the romance, he wondered to himself, the adventure, the thrill of traveling, of seeing new places? What was the point of going if everything was so predictable, so mapped out? He slowly began laughing to himself.

"Sam, I've already warned you about this unilateral laughter."

"Sorry. I was just thinking that Bogie in Casablanca has become Oprah at Planet Hollywood."

They both sat up as the latest in a series of casino ships in a town never much interested in the Vegas life style, made its way up the channel. It didn't seem too crowded. As they watched it go by, Edie remarked, "Do you think we will ever stop being target groups for somebody's schemes?"

"I don't know," said Sam, turning towards the cruise ship passengers heading up the gang plank, "but somebody sure hit the bull's eye with those folks."

Chapter 5

Seventh Inning Stretch

By now the calypso band had wrapped it up for the night. As they gathered their equipment in the mixture of municipal beige lighting and the big ship's overpowering security lights, the silhouettes of a few returning passengers could still be seen. Sam and Edie sat in the intimate shadow of the monster's stern.

If the white behemoth had not been in port that night, sitting on that dock would have been an uncomfortable experience. During cold front conditions, this was the windward side of the island. The Canadian air whistling across the open water would have seemed like the icy wind known as the "hawk" in Chicago – at least for our tropicalized heroes. But the cruise ship, like the "Great Wall" keeping out barbarians, blocked the northwest wind and made it a comfortable place to be.

The distant sound of vacation nightlife back on the street seemed light years away. With the sudden tranquility left by the band's absence, along with the protective shield which detoured the chilly air around them, neither of our protagonists seemed eager to leave. There was only one way back and that was through the minefields of revelry they had recently fled from. They were not ready for that assault yet.

Edie lay back once again, stretching elastically like a cat

that had just woken up. Sam had the urge to pounce on her, to cover her length with his sinewy body, but he now understood the foolishness of such a move. By now he realized this girl could not be seduced, that she could not be "made" with confident manly posturing. At this point in the game there was nothing to be done. Perhaps he could still "blow it," but something that could dazzle her or sweep her off her feet seemed not in play. When and if she was ready – she'd be the first to let him know. In a way, the pressure was off; it was out of his hands. Yeah, yeah, he said to himself, if only he could believe it. Somewhere along the line there'd be a moment of truth and it would be – he didn't want to think about it.

"Sam," her voice barged into his thoughts, "do you have any aspirations – something you'd really like to do or accomplish?"

Ha, he thought, as he unconsciously perused the full length of Edie's still tautly stretched body. He spoke in a muffled drone, as if he were talking to himself. "Boy, do I have aspirations."

Edie sat up and realized where Sam was at. In a way, she really did find it "cute." By now she knew there was nothing crass or insincere about this offbeat man. She was beginning to feel like a woman again, a woman being pursued by a man. It was beginning to feel good, as if she were returning to the realm of the living, as if she were returning to her true self again. "No Sam, I'm sorry, whatever our short term aspirations are – I can't say for now –"

"I can."

"I know, I know." She closed her eyes and breathed

deeply, wondering why this was all so difficult.

"Look, Edie, could you give me a capsule rundown of how this game is going, of where we might be at the moment?"

The tinkle of cruise ship rigging lightly floated onto the northern air. It was a soothing sound, a familiar sound of routine business. It calmed the moment. "Well, I'd say we've reached the seventh inning stretch. Take a break, relax. The finale is still ahead of us." The rigging continued chirping sweetly. "Sam," she said, perhaps trying to break the tension, "you're quite a sportsman, aren't you?"

Chapter 6

The Western Ethic

Sam turned his attention from the suckability of the feminine splendor by his side to the blackened night before him. He had always been a good athlete – not good enough to make a living at it – those guys were more like Gods than athletes – but always one of the best in the neighborhood. He couldn't imagine himself without some kind of sporting element in his life. As a middle-aged, post glory athlete, he'd taken up tennis, with which he faithfully frustrated himself on a regular basis.

"Yeah, I've played a little ball in my day. I've tracked down some long ones, shot a few hoops. I'll even serve an ace once in awhile. Perhaps the first ego gratification I ever had came from being an athlete." He tried to imitate Howard Cosell. "Yeah, I've grabbed for the glory, listened to the cheers, felt the thrill of victory and the agony of defeat – and believe me, my feet were in agony."

Edie shook her head. "Terrible." He cracked a sheepish smile and shrugged. She then remembered the time they'd spent in the park. "And the refereeing – what about that?"

"Wow, the refereeing." He peered into the water some 10 feet below his feet. The tide was going out, a fact which eluded our boy's consciousness as he reminisced about the years he'd spent as a referee. Of all the things he'd done with his life, this was probably the most demanding, most

175

competence intensive act he had ever involved himself with. And yet, unlike the adulation so easily garnered by a successful athletic performance, except for the very reduced circle of peers you worked with, the best a referee could hope for was to be totally ignored – and anything worse was the beginning of varying degrees of abuse and hostility.

"C'mon Sam, you don't want to talk about it?"

"No, no, I'll talk about it with anyone who'll listen. It's a fascinating subject."

"I'm listening."

Sam took a deep breath and rubbed his eyes. "You know Edie, I don't think there's a referee anywhere who doesn't wonder why he or she does such a thing." He furrowed his brow and continued to stare at the outgoing tide. "I suppose, more than anything, I love watching the kids play. They are at an age where they are almost to the border separating the foolishness of adolescence from the responsibility of being a man. In some ambiguous way, these basketball games could be seen as an initial brush with manhood."

"Cool."

Sam raised his gaze from the water and glanced to his left, mindlessly zeroing in on the lighted buoys marking the ship channel lost in the nocturnal darkness. His peripheral vision caught the movement of a calico cat sniffing out the culinary possibilities of a 50-gallon garbage drum. Her belly hung down flaccidly in mute evidence of a recent pregnancy. In spite of her street cat gauntness, she gracefully jumped to the rim of the drum and began foraging. Now there's an athlete, thought Sam.

"But that can't be all of it," he continued. "The abuse a

referee must take is not natural. It's something most people would not consider exposing themselves to and many of those who try last a few kiddy league games and no more. Everyone experiences some ill will behind their back – gossip and shit like that – but the idiot in stripes will be publically blamed for the most hellatious things done to the species. Hitler and Stalin will seem like one of the mischievous Simpson kids compared to that sightless dike-faggot moron who just whistled the local hero for a foul." He turned to his companion and spoke directly to her face. "It's amazing."

"So why do you do it?"

He leaned back slightly, supporting himself on his elbows as he blankly stared into the blackness beyond the dock. "Didn't you say something about not needing to be happy – or not needing, or something like that?"

"Did I?"

"Was it back on the wooden pier –I think it was still light out."

"Was that before or after the birth of Christ?"

"Hey, don't blame me."

"I know, I know." Edie leaned back on her elbows as well. "What's that got to do with refereeing?"

Sam caught a glimpse of the calico jumping down from the garbage drum. She quickly stole off into the darkness with some unidentified alley cat morsel pressed greedily between her teeth. After the Revolution, he thought, all the cats would have enough to eat – and there'd be no more simpletons on cruise ships or assholes in high school gymnasiums.

He suddenly sat up. His mind had cleared and his

thoughts flowed forth like a just opened fire hydrant. "You know Edie, dealing with glory, with praise, with adulation and flattery – anyone can do that. You really find out about someone when they have to deal with adversity, when someone has to beat back stupidity and senseless rage, when you have to be right when everyone else is wrong. Forget the glory, the fame, the hero worship. Forget trying to be wonderful. For almost all of us, trying to be wonderful only leads to failure and frustration. This needing to be special or heroic – it's the pursuit of an illusion. Go the other way. Seek not to need such praise and adulation. Happiness is being content with yourself, with not needing. A truly whole person doesn't need all this reinforcement from others –" he suddenly stopped, shook his head and again rubbed his eyes, "oh Jesus, listen to that crap."

Edie couldn't help but laugh. "No Sam," she momentarily went into a parody of his down island accent, "dot's cool, mon. I do remember saying something like that. The 'no needing' thing, the not-needing-to-be-happy-being-happy spiel. I think you expressed it better than I did."

She tried to remember when she had spoken those thoughts. Although they had only spent 1/3 of a day out of their whole lives together, the encounter had been so intense, so intellectually concentrated, it seemed as if they had passed through periods of history together.

"But Sam," she added pensively, "I think that position needs some modification."

"Oh God," he replied, throwing his head back and swooning comically, "you mean I've got it all wrong?"

"No, no – basically I agree –"

"Woo!" he said sarcastically, "that's a relief."

Our leading lady turned away impatiently, not having appreciated Sam's innocent but condescending attempt at humor. He realized he had offended her intelligence. He realized he could be an idiot. He realized this woman was more than a match for his own intellect. He realized this was why she so enthralled him. He realized he did not want to fail with her. He realized this was serious business. He realized a million different things at that moment.

"Look, Edie, that fly snuck right up on me. Please, I spit him out. I'm OK now." She turned to him shaking her head and smiling sadly. She'd forgiven him. "Go on Edie, you were saying –?"

"I was saying that basically I agree with you, but you can't completely negate this quest for achievement. That would be something like denying us our qualities as human beings. It would be something like denying nature its right to evolve. As human beings our egos need to be stroked somewhat – but I agree, our current way of life – how would you label it –?"

Sam cut in, "the western ethic?"

"Good. The western ethic has become unbalanced in this aspect, and the American version of it has even become more extreme. We stress this idea of individual glory, of competitive subjugation, beyond healthy limits. We have to strike a better balance here. We have become the extremists of ego. I suppose a bull crapping politician would call for a return to the center – I'm not a bull crapping politician – but why not? We need to egotistically return to the center."

Sam sat in dumbfounded rapture as he listened to her getting in her intellectual licks. If she played guitar, he thought, she'd be Roy Clark or B.B. King – or better yet, Casals or Segovia. "Gosh Edie, I'm not sure you're supposed to be so smart."

"Oh c'mon Sam – you're the referee, you know who you are. Nobody should intimidate you."

The bewitched cackles of squabbling gulls on the empty cruise ship berth to the south floated clearly on the dry winter air. The standard mirth of humans on vacation drifted dimly out from the city behind them. A light chop gently stroked the hull of "Her Royal Fucking Majesty." Sam and Edie sat on the dock. The Earth kept turning.

Chapter 7

Alex Karras

At this point in our story's emotional battle, after all that had been said; after all that had been done; after traveling such a long and arduous road, it would seem unlikely that the dreaded awkward silence would rear its frightening head once again – but, like some pesky weed that continues to invade your lawn in spite of all your efforts, our pair found themselves immersed in yet another of these uncomfortable interludes. It witnessed the fact that this game was not over, that the issue was still in doubt, that somebody still had to come up with that big hit to win the game.

Sam tried to save the day. "You know Edie –"

"You know Sam," she said cutting in, "you say 'you know Edie' a lot."

He laughed. "I never took Public Speaking 101 in college."

"That's OK. You don't have the face to be a newscaster anyway." The now familiar brooding expression etched an appearance in his face as he pondered the remark. His vulnerability bubbled to the surface, a vulnerability that, unknown to him, appealed to the feminine prey he longed for. Perhaps she was not aware of this either. "Oh God Sam," she added with a touch of scorn, "you gorillas are so stupid. Don't worry about your face. You were saying –?"

"You know Edie –" they laughed for a moment until he tried to continue. "I think what I aspire to –" he shrugged, not sure if he should go on.

"Go ahead, let it go."

"Well –"

"No," Edie broke in, "let me guess." She remembered the piece of paper in the park and his parody of "What's My Line?" "You want to be a writer, right?"

Sam looked away towards the lights blinking in the ship channel. The wind seemed to be dying and the sound of the ship's rigging had just about faded away. Maybe it would begin to warm up again. "How'd you get so smart?" he remarked, still looking towards the monotonous rhythms of the buoys.

"What's the problem? That stuff you showed me in the park was quite good."

"Yeah – I guess." He turned and looked directly at her. "But it's hard to feel worthy, there is so little encouragement. Nobody takes you seriously. Writing a book would almost be a presumptuous act."

"Fucken A," she said angrily, "you're acting like some whimpering dog that needs to have his head patted. Jesus! Weren't we just talking about this? You don't mind being accused of idiocy on the basketball court, do you?" He tried to defend himself but she cut him off. "Shut up and listen. If you are going to worry about what the fog brains think of you, then you should aspire to be a moron." She paused, shook her head and let forth with one of her more robust horse snorts. "Have you heard this one Sam? 'Try our thin and crispy crust, our deep dish cavatini is a must'."

"Some kind of pizza commercial," he said sullenly,

accepting his tongue lashing just like a whimpering dog, "isn't it?"

"Someone is actually receiving accolades, self satisfaction, remuneration in material wealth and God only knows what else for that poetic excrement. I've seen pictures in art museums – a line here, a dot there – and curtains strung across Grand and not so Grand Canyons. Who knows, maybe they are great works of art. What's-His-Name Dershowitz, the lawyer from hell – he's an actor! And LeBron James –and some skin head, blow hard wrestler became Governor. The other night I saw the promo for a new movie release; it was billed as 'the film event of the year'. Is that the best they can do? I swear, the next time anyone says 'Oh my God' just as the volcano blows, or the ship sinks, or the meteor heads for Disneyland, I'm going to walk straight to the box office and demand my money back. Alex Karras thought he'd reached his zenith with his head in the mud on Thanksgiving morning –"

"How do you know about Alex Karras?"

"I already told you," she said impatiently, "I have older brothers, but don't interrupt." She shook her head and breathed deeply, letting it out with weary frustration. "Who the hell isn't an actor? Who the hell isn't an artist? Everyone has something artistic within them, but they never find out because they are put on the assembly line where they get time and a half to barely pay the rent, frozen foods, and a frozen brain for their efforts. You want to be a writer Sam? Just shut up and write."

The gulls continued squawking on the neighboring dock. The red and green lights mysteriously lit the marine highway into port. They sat silently for about 20 seconds. "I suppose," said Sam, breaking the silent interlude, "if we were players in the usual cinema fodder, this is where I'd say 'thanks, I needed that'."

"Sam, I have to pee."

Chapter 8

A Foreign Country

We now find our hero standing in front of an upscale timeshare resort –The Carriage House – which has occupied one side of Jackson Street's waterfront dead end for the last 14 years. It had a spacious, well-appointed lobby, which helped justify the daily fortune it took to stay there. The floor was immaculately paved in brick colored slabs of smooth Spanish tile, the walls were tastefully garnished with local works of art, the lighting was indirectly soft, and the staff was meticulously dressed in matching tropical shirts. The suites above were equally plush, luxuriously appointed with the pastel colored splendor of tropical wicker taste; elegant, light, relaxing – the perfect getaway for the man and woman who had it all. Topping it off was the obligatory Jacuzzi and a splendid view of the harbor with the well-marketed sunsets provided by the resort's westward orientation.

Some people, thought Sam, had to pay stacks of money for everything they did, even to watch the sunset. They somehow did not feel fulfilled if they couldn't spend the money others didn't have. He remembered standing in the pro shop at the tennis courts just a few days before, leafing through a tennis magazine. An ad for a space age racquet caught his attention, mainly because it was trumpeting a price tag of more than $400. He wondered why its manufacturer was so eager to quote such an elevated price. Just that morning he had noticed a large, meticulous sign in front of a resort development currently under construction; it seemed to be bragging that their homes were "starting at $400,000." As he wended his way through his stay on this planet, it seemed increasingly evident the more expensive something got – at least with regard to "luxury" – the less return one received. Certainly, a $100,000 Mercedes was a better car than a $1,000 used car in good working order – but 100 times better? Sam suddenly realized that for some people this elevated price was their identity, their persona; the exaggerated cost *was* the reason they bought something.

By now the time was closing in on one o'clock in the morning. Although the impala herd had thinned out some, South Isle was known for its partying mentality and the downtown area was still bustling with vacationers escaping the routine of their daily lives. Sam the "local" stood in front of the elegant resort and took it all in. He tried to remember what had stood here before the global economy had intervened in this part of the world. For some inexplicable quirk of the human mind, from the inland side of the port area he could not visualize anything of what used to be here. He vaguely saw – were there some oil tanks, a fuel dock? He shook his head and shrugged. Nope – the image was just about gone now, lost forever, buried under the glitzy timeshare resort scam now occupying the site. In spite of the majestic conceit of its current dominance, it too, thought Sam, would be gone someday.

As he continued scanning the contemporary scene, he felt that now familiar yearning for those pre-Carriage

House days. He wondered if this nostalgia was just a smokescreen for the inevitable loss of one's youth – and the cynicism that came with it – or had things really been better then? The island was a real place then, with real people doing real jobs. But tourism was a genuine reality too – in fact, tourism had always been an important part of South Isle's existence. But this Global-Economy-Madison-Avenue tourism was a different animal. There was something about it that was not entirely honest, that was affected, that was forced, like when you were a kid and you had to kiss an aunt or uncle you didn't like. This was mandatory fun, mass marketed happiness. It was not permissible to not have a good time, even if they lost your luggage, or over booked your flight, or took you out snorkeling on a windy day. Yeah, sure, we had a great time.

Standing in front of the Carriage House, Sam began to feel that out of place alienation he had felt when they first hit Jackson Street an hour or two before. In the old days, this was his town, all of it. But the downtown area had become a foreign country for most residents, a place you only ventured into to make a living.

"What's up Sam?" Edie had gone into the Carriage House to take a leak. Her return had startled our hero, so immersed in his thoughts that even his desperate pursuit of our fair lady had momentarily been pushed aside.

"Woo!" He twitched as if he had touched a live wire.

"Sorry, I didn't mean –"

"No, no, that's OK."

"Gosh, where were you?"

He stretched his arms over his head and shook himself like a dog who'd just come out of the water. "Oh God, nowhere I haven't been before. What's up? Feel better now?"

"Yeah, much better. Look, Sam, I just saw something in the bar that I want to show you. I could use a cup of coffee too."

Chapter 9

The High Priced Spread

The Carriage House had a lovely bar-restaurant with a dominant view of the harbor and the wide expanse of ocean and mangrove islands which stretched off to the western horizon. It was known as the Sundowner. Unfortunately, its northwestern exposure was diametrically opposed to maximizing the climatic conditions of the island. During the incessant heat and humidity of the warm part of the year, what relief there was arrived on the breeze from the southeast quadrant, a breeze that was thoroughly obliterated by the bulk of the resort's structure. In the winter, the cold fronts came whistling in across the Great Plains like an arrow heading for its target, and the Sundowner was its bull's eye. After a few initial years of commercial disappointment, they had decided to enclose the area, but at least they had done it in a tasty way; the beautiful view could still be seen through a wide sweep of sliding glass that could be closed when winter made one of its half-hearted forays into the northern tropics.

At this time of day, as Sam and Edie sat on bar stools cozily positioned around a small, high riding table in front of the sliding glass, there wasn't much to see in the nocturnal black out. A few lights from the construction site on Oil Island – henceforth known as "Paradise Isle" – hung in the darkened canvas like low-lying stars. A bow side view of the cruise ship just to the south vaguely emerged from the night like a huge mirage. Our daunting pair hovered over 2 cups of coffee and gazed blankly into the darkness beyond.

In keeping with the resort's elegance, the cups were sturdy pieces of real china, flanked by dainty napkins emblazoned tastefully with the establishment's logo – a gracefully curved palm tree set before a setting sun. Two delicate spoons for sugar sat carelessly on the smooth surface of the round table.

"Boy," said Sam, a bit exasperated, "three dollars and 75 cents for a cup of coffee?"

Edie examined the cup she was drinking from. It too had the palm tree logo on its side. "I really like drinking coffee from a real porcelain cup."

Our boy was still not convinced. "Well," he said grudgingly, "it beats Styrofoam, I'll give you that."

And the coffee was good; hot, rich – maybe not $3.75 rich, but somebody had to pay for the overhead of this place.

They sipped in silence, letting the smooth liquid course through their bodies. Suddenly, Edie saw something reflected on the glass of one of the sliding doors. "Oh, I almost forgot. I wanted to show you something." She turned slightly and looked towards the bar. "You see that guy who looks like he could be the Ambassador to France?"

Sam turned and saw an elegant man, 60-ish, with a brilliant shock of perfectly barbered silver hair. He wore a dark gray suit over a pale blue shirt. The tie was navy blue with the barest hint of a few green stripes. He seemed bored as he sipped a rum and coke. The stool next to him was momentarily unoccupied, an untouched vodka and cranberry attesting to the absence of somebody. "Yeah, what about him?"

"He's wearing a double knit suit."

Sam laughed lustily as he remembered her promise to point such a thing out. It seemed centuries ago, as if they'd been married for years. "What makes it a double knit suit?"

"It has to do with the fabric. If we get closer I could point it out."

"That's OK; I think we can pass on that." Sam took a sip of his coffee and continued to look at the well-tailored gentleman. "He seems a bit out of place here, doesn't he?" Edie looked ironically at Sam's ketchup stained Marlins jersey and burst out laughing. He quickly realized the humor in his remark and joined her in a few moments of unrefined giddiness. When they had finally emptied the laughter tank, he added, "Hey, that jacket you're wearing is about 10 sizes too big." They laughed some more and finally went back to their coffee.

But Sam's remark was not entirely incorrect. Although the Sundowner was considered quite elegant in the island's bar-restaurant hierarchy, the town itself was marketed as a very "laid back" resort. It was the kind of place where you could supposedly kick back and relax, traffic jams and wall to wall people aside. This "laid back" idea really didn't exist anymore as the Chamber of Commerce jackals frantically sought their share of the tourist carcass; but that was the marketing device. In a way, as we've said earlier in this tale, South Isle had become a caricature of what it used to be.

The smattering of customers still in the bar reflected this idea. Most of them were dressed casually but expensively. There was an abundance of white or pastel colored cotton pants accompanied by wide collared tropical shirts with lively prints of exotic flowers or lazy palms. But the island's Bohemian-off beat history still yielded a bit of acceptability to the sloppy disdain for fashion exhibited by our couple. It would not be unreasonable to consider the aristocratic elegance of our distinguished, silver haired gentleman to be more out of place in this bar. It was obvious he did not understand this town. He seemed to have mistaken South Isle for Palm Springs or West Palm Beach.

Sam was still looking at him when a platinum blond in high heel shoes emerged from the lady's room and made her way back to the stool next to him. She was dressed in a full-length, silvery dress that clung to her superb body like a piece of saran wrap. Her slimness did not preclude the firm curve of a magnificent, high riding butt and her breasts had the haughty conceit of the finest money could buy. Her leisurely stroll across the room had attracted every male eye in the place, as if she were a suspicious blip on a wartime radar screen.

"Wow!'" exclaimed Sam, as he followed her across the room, "that must be the high priced spread, eh?"

Edie had nothing to say. She knew she had no right to resent Sam's infatuation with this sizzling example of feminine allure, but somehow – it put her in a darkish kind of mood. Wasn't it just this shallowness that had disappointed her with men after all these years? On the other hand – was she feeling a bit jealous? Maybe that was good? She was still so confused about all this.

It was almost impossible to not think of Marilyn Monroe and Edie did not want to end up like Marilyn Monroe. "I guess she has to pay for those tits somehow," she said sarcastically, perhaps more annoyed with the woman for hire than with Sam the lech. She resented her for degrading all women.

But really – and Edie knew this – there was no one to blame. The Gillette Gods were still firmly in control.

Chapter 10

Like Polishing a Candelabra

*E*die looked away from Marilyn and the Ambassador and stared blankly into the night. Much as she tried, there still seemed to be a bit of "attitude" in play. She knew she was acting irrationally, that there was something not quite right in her thinking, something that had made it almost impossible for her to succumb to a man. She had a problem.

Sam was oblivious to this as he continued to examine the out of place Palm Springs couple. Unbeknownst to Edie, the erotic qualities of the painted lady were no longer his motivation. He was now examining the human condition and what he saw was not too flattering. Although from a geographic standpoint Marilyn and the Ambassador could be considered together, it was easy to see that from an emotional sense there were virtually no lines of communication. Each continued to sip their respective drinks, isolated in their own worlds, even the simple task of polite chatter seemingly beyond their capabilities. Their relationship had all the romance of a shit stained diaper.

"I paid for sex only one time in my life," said Sam, as he turned back towards the sliding glass door and peered into the darkness beyond it. "It was in the Dominican Republic."

Our girl sat silently, staring stonily into the nothingness. For the first time, Sam realized he had somehow annoyed her. My God, he thought, I've hardly even touched her, we've spent a few hours together, and already we are having a bit of a tiff. He wondered if he could ever really make a go of it with a lady.

"C'mon Edie, what's the problem?"

"Oh, I'm just being a dickhead." She took a sip of coffee and wiped her mouth with the cutesy napkin. "Sometimes I think there's not another man anywhere I can really get close to. I expect too much."

Sam closed his eyes and rubbed his forehead. "I was just thinking the same thing." It was getting late.

"Gosh," said Edie wearily, "we have so much in common." They chuckled softly in a forced kind of way, as if some kind of melancholy fatalism had permeated the environment, as if all their attempts at romantic fulfillment were doomed. Edie tried to resolve the situation. "You were saying – something about the Dominican Republic?"

"I was down there once and it was the only time I ever paid for sex –if you could call it that."

"You really didn't pay?"

"No, no," he laughed at her naivety, "I paid alright, but I'm not sure you could call it sex."

"Why, was she ugly or no good?"

"No, quite the contrary, she was very attractive." He could still see her smooth, milk chocolate skin and her clean, Belafonte-like features. The Dominican was covered with girls just like her and it seemed like almost all of them were for hire. "The problem was that it was a business transaction and her lack of interest – and she tried to fake it, believe me – could not be overlooked."

"What happened?"

"She tried to get me hard with her hand, but it was like

– I don't know – it was so mechanical, like she was polishing a candelabra or something. I gave her the money and sent her away."

Edie shook her head and sighed. The whole idea of selling herself like that was something her respectable upbringing could not come close to understanding. "It just seems so horrible. What a sad life to live."

They retreated silently into their own thoughts, alternating sips of coffee with blank stares into the darkness beyond the glass doors. Both of them noticed the reflection of Marilyn and the Ambassador as they got up to leave the bar. They turned to watch as the red carpet couple made their way towards the exit. The aristocratic gentleman offered her his arm as they walked out, which she accepted like a trained zombie. There was not the least bit of emotional energy between them. The old boy had decided, thought Sam, the time for ejaculation had arrived, in much the same way he might decide to brush his teeth or take a dump.

Sam mused out loud, "I suppose this is the other side of the coin."

"What do you mean?"

"Well," our boy pondered the situation a bit more, "is their idea of sex any more ridiculous than what we are torturing ourselves with right now?" He motioned with his head towards the doorway through which our sex-as-commerce couple had just passed. He then looked at Edie and continued. "Weren't you the one who mentioned something about the absurd 'cathedral' –I think that was the word you used – we've built around the sexual act?"

"Cathedral?"

"Yeah – and what – I quote – 'middle class rubbish' it was."

"That definitely sounds like something I would say."

"Whereas people like you or I were taught to exaggerate the importance of this act, to give it some kind of sacred meaning, Silver and the Flashy Dame give it almost no importance at all, as if it were just one of many bodily functions. Whereas we've just about killed the organic pleasure of it all in angst, they've killed it in routine tedium."

"So what's the answer?"

Sam looked into the now empty coffee cup. He noticed a pasty residue of sugar clinging to the bottom. He took the little sugar spoon, scooped some of it out, and wiped it clean with his tongue. "I think that is what we are trying to figure out, isn't it?"

Edie took her last gulp of coffee. She wiped her mouth with the back of her fingers. "Sam, let's call a cab. The ball is definitely in my court. The rest of the evening is under my supervision."

Part 3

Chapter 1

Maybe

They hailed a cab in front of the Carriage House and headed out of the downtown area. Edie had told the driver where to go before getting in the car, leaving our hero in the dark.

"Where are we going?"

"Just sit back and relax."

Just one block off of Jackson Street the bluster and revelry of vacationing nightlife was left behind, replaced by the soothing darkness of the Old Barrio streets. It felt good to be out of there, as if they had returned to their natural habitat. It was a bit after 1:30 and there was hardly any traffic at all. The old Victorian homes and dense tropical foliage stood eerily in the dim street light, like something from an Emily Bronte novel. The cab found no resistance as it sped up the main street out of the Old Barrio.

When Edie had suggested the cab, Sam found himself in an immediate state of anxiety. He felt as if something was imminent, that the game was about to be decided. Upon entering the cab, he felt a nervous tingle all over his body as well as what seemed to be a rise in his body temperature. Unbeknownst to him, these were the embryonic beginnings of a bodily state ending in fainting, though he never came close to arriving at such. He was lucid enough to know it was not in his hands anymore, that the woman had taken over, as he always knew she eventually would. His mind began to roll possibilities over in a confused haze of uncertainty and desperation. Maybe she had told the driver to go to his house and drop him off? Good night, thanks for a wonderful evening – oh fuck, not that! Maybe she would come in with him? Maybe they'd go to her place? Maybe – maybe, maybe. He was reminded of an ancient pop tune from the early days of rock and roll. He could not remember the group that had sung it.

But as the cab made its way out of the Old Barrio he realized that "none of the above" had taken over the moment. Our boy began to lowly sing the old tune, in the a cappella clearness he remembered so well. "**Maybe, maybe, may-ay-beee** – do you remember that one?"

"Try it again."

"**Maybe, maybe, may-ay-bee**."

The cab was stopped at a light. The neon blaze of an all night convenience store degraded the ambiance. Edie shook her head. "No, I don't know it."

"You're probably too young."

The light changed and the car hurried on, leaving the crass neon in its wake. The lesser personalities of the New Barrio's residential neighborhoods were unconsciously left behind, as the ugly moles of the beach side condos began to rear their heads towards the south. The road passed through a short canyon of such buildings and abruptly turned to the left. They were now on the beach road running along the ocean.

South Isle's longest beach ran for more than a mile along the south side of the island. After about a ¼ mile, the condos across the street from the beach gave way to a dense tangle of mangrove swamp fronting the salt ponds lying behind them. Some recent hurricanes had thinned the mangrove out, leaving the salt ponds visible from the road for the first time Sam could ever remember. If not for the intervention of Federal and State ecological agencies, Lento and his gang of dialing-for-dollars henchmen would have probably filled in these tidal ponds with a backdrop of hotels and condos. Beyond the salt ponds, to the northeast, stood the island's small commercial airport, which would not open until five in the morning. The red light on top of its control tower could be seen in the distance. It was very dark out there.

Just before the road turned back towards the left – or north – to link up with the rest of the island's road system, Edie told the driver to stop. By now the beach had run out and only a wide, seaside promenade – what the Cubans call a *"malecon"* – separated the ocean from the road. By the time the sun came up, there would already be a smattering of joggers, skaters, walkers and cyclists whose numbers would increase as the morning wore on. But for now, the sidewalk was deserted and the traffic on the road minimal.

Our pair stepped out into the inky darkness and the cab sped off in search of more financial prey, leaving them alone under the vast heavenly dome above. The lack of light provided a magnificent planetarium-like celestial theater. The clear winter sky bristled with stars, so much so that the Milky Way, with its thicker concentration of light, could be easily delineated in the stellar map.

Edie had carefully chosen the site. They sat down on a bench which pointed them out to sea. Although she was not a "Luddite," she did not carry her modern communication device with her. She did not feel the need to be that "connected," and for some inexplicable reason, she'd have bet confidently that Sam was similarly unarmed. As a result, she had chosen this bench because it had a pay phone next to it – a pay phone that she knew still worked – ready to be called upon for the return trip back to town. They stretched out and relaxed, taking in the breathtaking panorama above and beyond. The ever-present navigational lights blinked eternally on the sea, this time marking the reef which protected the island's southern flank 6 miles out. It had taken them 10 minutes to get there –but what they had left behind seemed light years away.

Chapter 2

Nothing to Write About

They sat for awhile – 5 minutes, 10, who was counting. Finally, Sam felt the urge to break the spell. "This is really nice."

"Sometimes when I feel restless, or uptight, or –I don't know, when I can't sleep, I come up here on my bicycle to watch the sunrise."

"Does that happen often?"

Does it happen often? Lately, she seemed to be doing it more frequently. "Well – it has been happening more often – but more because I'm beginning to like it. There's something about the sunrise that the sunset can't match. No commercial parasites are selling the sunrise. It's more private, more personal. It's a beginning rather than an end. The air is cleaner, more easy to see through. There are more birds and critters about. The sounds are crisper, sharper. There is a sacrifice to be made in order to experience it. The sunrise is more genuine, more honest, more heartfelt. It inspires me artistically, spiritually –"

Sam thought of the frangipane flower she had put in her waist purse earlier in the evening. He could not help but ask the same question he'd asked then. "Are you an artist?"

She shrugged and gazed out to sea. The dim lights of a shrimp boat making its way back to Hog Island just to the east caught her attention. A whole string of shrimp boat lights could be seen stretched along the south side of the island, anchored in the lee of the northern wind until the weather improved enough to go fishing again. "Something like that."

He thought back to when Edie had lectured him on "art," when she had figuratively slapped him in the face. "You know Edie –" he realized he'd said it again and they both laughed. "I just can't help it."

"That's OK, what's the difference?" With the wind blowing off shore, there was almost no sound of water lapping the sea wall in front of them. The only sound was the far off putt-putt of the shrimper on its way back to port. "What was it you want me to know?"

"I was thinking of that lecture you gave me on 'art'." He stopped and laughed to himself, thinking back on what he was about to tell our fair lady.

"There you go again –" she said, sarcastically irritated.

"No, no, I was just thinking about this job I worked yesterday – was it yesterday?"

"Probably not. It kind of feels like yesterday is still today – or vice versa. You can blame it on me if you'd like."

It had been a long haul, no doubt about it. Sam rubbed the bridge of his nose and continued. "Anyhoo, I was working this job – I say, Edie, can you guess what job it was?"

She answered immediately. "Earning enough cash to have enough grub, etc., etc."

"You are good Edie, really good." She smiled and batted her eyelashes at him playfully. Sam went on. "Anyway, such job creates some forgettable moments. For instance, painting the walls of some suburban golfer's reward for his prudent investment strategies, which have given him the means to schlep his two-child family down here for a week every year."

"Schlep? You must have Jewish friends too, eh?"

"They're everywhere. My first girl friend here was Jewish. When I was in high school we used to seek out the Jewish girls because they were supposed to be easy."

Edie laughed and shook her head. "I had a Jewish boy friend once who said they did the same thing, but with the gentile girls."

Now they both laughed. "I guess," said Sam, still somewhat giddy, "we are all just schmegeg – schmega – what was that word you used?"

"Schmeggegies."

"Right, no matter who you are, it's a world full of schmeggegies."

They sat for a moment, listening to the dim, rhythmic sound of the shrimp boat plodding towards Hog Island. "So Sam, you were painting the golfer's vacation getaway –"

"Right. So there I was, and I'm trying to paint, and my brain is saying 'what time is it?, let's take a break, we can finish tomorrow,' such brain being assaulted by an evil smelling primer persistently curling up my nostrils, such nostrils now beginning to twitch and flutter under the relentless attack of the carcinogenic answer to the bare walls before me – woo!"

"Ahh," chimed in Edie, "the things we do for grub, clothes and protection from the elements." And for sex, she thought to herself, as she gazed out at the endless sea, at 2 in the morning, on a bench at the end of the world, on a winter night in the tropics. "What's that got to do with 'art'?"

"I generally work such jobs with Bush the Red, house painter extraordinaire and middle class refugee cum laude. While working yesterday – or whenever – Bush noticed a mural of sorts hanging upon the wall to be primed. It was a rather large affair, perhaps 4' by 6', festooned colorfully with a liberal amount of shapes, lines, dots, swirls, splups, splops, drops and other assorted forms and shapes, the type of thing that might sell for 3-jillion dollars under the gavel of some starched English gentleman encased in a tuxedo."

"Did you like it?"

"Not for 3-jillion dollars, but yes, I liked it. I found it much more visually pleasing than an oil refinery. But Bush, it seems, has a finer appreciation for art than I do. Not being as impressed as I was, he picked up a 4" paint brush and dipped it delicately into the soft blue being dabbed here and there in the soon to be beautiful kitchen. With this bluely tipped instrument of creativity, Bush the Red placed himself about two feet in front of the mural and, like a champion dart thrower, deftly wristed a light indigo shower onto the canvas. He examined his work for a moment, nodded smugly to himself and muttered something like 'yes, that's better'."

"I bet that painting is worth 4 jillion now."

Sam smiled and shook his head, marveling at what his co-worker had done. He wished he had the *"cojones" to do* something like that. He wondered if the mural's artist would have noticed the difference. He wondered why he wondered about everything. "You know Edie, when Bush did that I couldn't believe it. I said, 'Hey! What are you doing?' But he just ignored me, as if I weren't there. He stepped back, framed the picture between his hands, and said, 'it needed some blue', and returned to what he was doing."

A solitary car made its way up the beach road towards our couple. As it smoothly slid by, the muddled sound of pop music could be heard fading into the distance. Both Sam and Edie turned to watch as it sped off around the bend in the road leading towards the other side of the island. When the red taillights had disappeared from view, Edie remarked, "Well, Sam, if Bush is such an artist, just think what a great writer you are."

He stared blindly into the starry stew above. A shooting star plummeted towards the invisible horizon beyond the reef. "Wow, did you see it?"

"I've already seen 2 of them," she said calmly, looking at him as he continued to scan the sky. She awaited his response, not letting him off the hook.

"What do I write about?"

"What's the difference? Write about tonight."

That well known brooding quality returned to our boy's face. He dropped his gaze and looked at Edie. "So far there's nothing to write about."

She turned away and looked out over the blackened sea plain. The dim putt-putt of the shrimp boat heading to Hog Island was almost gone now. She turned back towards the west, examining the darkness in that direction. A fuzzy conglomerate of lights could be seen back towards the ship channel. It was her "Royal Fucking Majesty" leaving South Isle in search of its next generic stop in "paradise." "I'm trying the best I can" was all she could think of saying.

Chapter 3

Dennis Rodman

*S*am was on the verge of losing his patience. He felt the urge to directly confront her, to scold her for her Byzantine, mind fucked, Rube Goldberg inability to simplify something she had obviously made way too complicated. For a brief instance he almost hated her; he wanted to get in her face and shout *what the hell is wrong with you! I get hard, you get wet, we both moan and groan for awhile, hallelujah!*

But he didn't. Like a tennis player who had just gotten a bad call and had to compose himself and keep playing, he stayed the course and kept his mouth shut. But he felt as if he were failing. What did he have to do? Why is it that some men had so much confidence, that some men melted feminine resistance like a hot sun on an ice cream cone? Perhaps he was wrong about Edie; perhaps she was more conventional than she seemed to be; perhaps she had to be boldly conquered, just like so many other women. Should he grab her and force his kisses upon her? He'd already tried that, clumsily, as usual, but maybe now –

"Look, Sam, one of the shrimp boats is leaving." While our boy had been immersed in his own goulash of emotional desperation, Edie had been miles away. He shook his head and smiled inwardly, realizing his little fit of anxiety had not been shared by his companion. He felt like an idiot. It suddenly dawned on him that whenever he felt like an idiot, it almost always had to do with a woman.

Sam looked out to sea and saw the boat Edie was referring to. Only its lights could be seen in the darkness, moving slowly but implacably off to the west, towards Mexico or wherever it was they found the shrimp moving. "That's a good sign," he said, "it means the weather is going to get better."

He felt better too, knowing his momentary loss of composure had not been perceived by the object of his pursuit. It relaxed him just enough to say something he might not have said otherwise as he tried to woo this special feminine prize. As he said it, he had no idea that it would lead to the fork in the road where this epic tale would be resolved. "Sometimes," he said innocently, "I have to wonder what's going on with women these days."

The remark caught Edie by surprise, and she immediately got defensive. "With women? What about men?"

Sam knew right away he had touched an exposed wire. Edie fell into a feminine – what? sub-culture? – he had now become familiar with: women who didn't trust men. They had been sincere in their love for their previous mates but the "groin brains" of their men had betrayed them. They were like street dogs with strangers, suspicious and leery of the whole thing. He'd even known some women who dabbled in lesbian relationships after a lifetime of hetero love. He wondered about the sincerity of these forays, or were they simply spiteful reactions to the disappointments they'd had with men? He wondered if the whole "gay" thing in our society, which seemed to have grown in his lifetime, was more than just people being able to "come out," but a reaction to the difficulties of living the conventional, monogamous lifestyle so glorified by the status quo. He wondered if there might be some algebraic equation stating that "decaying heterosexual relationships = increasing homosexual relationships." He began to feel stupid trying to theorize about such subterranean human feelings. If science could not figure these things out –

"Don't lay it on women Sam." Edie was not to be appeased. "What about men?"

Sighing heavily, he looked to the stars above. He knew her ill will was somewhat justified, but he also knew her loyalty to her gender was perhaps simplifying the whole thing. He often felt as if women were not seeing the complete picture.

"Look, Edie, I'm not going to deny that men are jerks. I'll even admit that when it comes to gender, we are the world leaders in being jerks."

"Thanks."

"But let's be reasonable here. There is a Newtonian quality with regard to everything that happens between men and women. If men have taken to being jerks these days, it most likely is a reaction to whatever it is you guys are putting forth. None of this is conscious, but whatever it is we are <u>all</u> buying into has created the current situation. Nobody is off the hook."

Edie was still not appeased. "Oh c'mon," she said angrily, "we're not the ones generally ruining relationships with our clits as you guys do with your dicks. We're not the ones physically abusing people. We're not the ones not paying child support –"

"Hold it! Hold it!" Sam held up his hands, requesting a truce. He now understood that what was about to take place on that bench, under the dwarfing influence of the clearly seen universe above, would be the culminant episode in this drama. Whatever it was that was keeping them from emotionally and physically coming together; whatever gender tension still keeping the road to erotic surrender blocked, was about to be put in play. The nitty-gritty had arrived. Either the war would be won on that bench, or no one would get out alive. "Believe me," he went on, "I'm on your side. You think my life with women has been satisfactory in the last few years? You think I'm getting what I need?" She was going to reply, but he cut her off. "No. I'm in the same boat you are. I'm not looking for some homemaker to decorate my house and cook me the perfect quiche every night. I'm all for women wanting all the options anyone else wants in life. My God, that would sure make you all much more interesting." His rival – and at that moment, rivals is what they had become – rolled her eyes and looked away towards the west. "But you know Edie," this time nobody saw the humor in the oft repeated expression, "I'm not that crazy about your solutions."

Edie did not reply. She focused in on the lights of the big cruise ship steaming out the channel. It was moving so slowly in the universal darkness that its progress could not be seen. It was no more than a far off lump of light.

There was a thickness to the silence that seemed to engulf them, as if they were in a claustrophobic cave without light rather than insignificant dots in the vast celestial panorama. Edie continued to stare out to sea.

"Edie, have you ever heard of the sport of girl's basketball?"

She kept staring at the ship channel, away from Sam, still simmering in her own emotional stew. She really wasn't seeing or looking at anything. She didn't bother to turn around as she spoke. "Girl's basketball?" she replied coldly, "I thought girls played basketball, just like men."

"They do now, but it wasn't always like that."

She continued staring away from Sam, out into the nothingness. "What's that have to do with anything?"

"Perhaps it is necessary for someone to explain this thing called girl's basketball, because it is just about gone from our memory. It is the whooping crane of athletic competition, doomed for extinction." Edie shrugged, showing little interest. Sam plowed on. "You see, back in that ill defined era known as the 'old days', the guardians of our culture – Jaycees, Kiwanis-Lions Club honchos, educators, PTA biggies, religious shamans and other respectable torch bearers –felt it wrong for girls to go around abusing themselves the way boys do. So they invented a game of basketball which differed somewhat from the male stampeding we are all so familiar with. Hoping to spare us the sight of the nation's young virgins – in those days, some of them still were –" Edie grunted sourly, "being gouged, elbowed, wrestled, trampled and laid out in the barbaric male fashion, the following game was devised: two teams of 6 opposed each other. Three players on each team were designated as defensive players and 3 as offensive players. The defensive and offensive players could only operate on their half of the court." He stopped to see if Edie was listening. "Does any of this, my dear friend, ring a bell for you?"

She finally turned and looked at him, still out of sorts.

"What's this have to do with anything?"

"Edie, you're the one who was demanding patience, weren't you?"

She nodded. "OK, touché." A car approached from the opposite direction from where they'd come. The angle of its headlights momentarily glared right on them. When it had passed, our girl explained, "believe it or not, now that you mention it, I can dimly remember my mom having played such a game." She scrunched her face in thought, trying to conjure up an image. "There was a photo in the family album – my mom is in a silly long dress with the rest of her teammates gathered around a basketball –" She snorted, shrugged and relaxed. "Oh God, it's hard for me to think of my mother as a basketball player – she's kind of short."

Sam was relieved. She had returned to some semblance of peaceful coexistence. "Anyway," he went on, "in the current ill defined era known as 'nowadays', girls have decided they want to play basketball just like boys do. I don't find this to be a horrible thing. It's a lot better than an oil spill in Alaska."

Edie snorted sarcastically. "Now there's a progressive attitude."

"Thank you," he replied, equally sarcastic, "but I have to admit, I would find it far more positive if women were interested in having men play girl's basketball."

A few hundred yards into the darkness, another shrimp boat began moving off to the west, but the hidden meaning behind its departure was not on our couple's minds. "Where are you going with all this Sam? I still don't get it."

"Look, you're the one who correctly accused men of being jerks –"

"Hold it – you're the one who said that."

"Yes, but with your prodding and your blessing."

Edie sat silently for a moment, pondering the situation. "OK, we're agreed – men are jerks."

"And what is the female solution to all this?"

She was getting impatient with the game. "You tell me," she snapped.

"To play basketball just like men do."

"There's a metaphor or analogy here, right?"

Sam noticed the departing shrimp boat. The weather was still chilly and there was no sign of the warmer, more humid southerly breezes. Maybe he was just looking for a better place to anchor out? He wondered if a Bible Belt shrimper, with his southern accent and bottle of Jack would ever find himself in the kind of romantic embroilment him and Edie were now agonizing through. What exactly was "love" for them? Who knows? He returned to the task at hand. "Look, I completely agree the traditional female role has become somewhat archaic in the modern world. I respect the current feminine unrest. But this same environment has made the traditional bread winning-hunter role equally archaic. These male-female divisions of labor have become far less relevant in these rancid days of Gillette Gods and –" he stopped abruptly, his expressive eyes wide open. "My God, I just had a revelation."

"I wait with baited breath."

"I think I just figured out the person who currently personifies the course of the 'western ethic' most."

"Who?"

"Dennis Rodman."

Chapter 4

The Big Gamble

"Dennis Rodman?" said Edie. "You mean the basketball player with all the hairdos and tattoos and rings through his nose and all that?"

"Yeah, the he-man athlete who likes to dress up like a woman."

They sat for awhile in silence, trying to digest such an eccentric thought. The magnificent sweep of a small part of the infinite universe stood in mute silence above, as if it too were awaiting some kind of explanation. There was no more movement amongst the shrimp boats. There was hardly any wind. The road behind remained empty. Only the navigational lights out near the reef continued to go about their business, dutifully marking the way in the invisible night.

"Dennis Rodman?" repeated Edie.

Sam could not help but mull over his statement, trying to explain it to himself. It was a feeling that had come upon him suddenly. "Well," he mumbled insecurely, trying to make some sense of it, "all philosophical generalizations – and to say Dennis Rodman is some kind of societal wind vane is certainly such –are usually too broad a brush stroke to be considered a Gospel-like rendition of fact –"

"Yeah," intervened our heroine, "not even the Gospel can be considered a Gospel-like rendition of fact."

"And least of all the Gospel," said Sam, as their laughter broke the tension of their emotional battle, as if both sides were regrouping and preparing for a final onslaught. "OK," he went on, "poor choice of words. Let's just say the broad generalization embodied in my Rodman comment, although it lacks any true empirical reason to give it any credence, might still contain an intuitive feel for something that makes sense. It might not be the exact answer to a puzzling riddle, in this case" –he paused trying to get it right, "the riddle of where our society is going, or even the human condition in general –"

"Boy!" Edie could not help but interrupt. "Quite a big chew we are biting off here, don't you think?"

Sam looked upwards, into the star strewn heavens above, and spread his arms majestically like Moses acknowledging the presence of his adulating tribe. "I feel inspired," he spoke with mock drama, "in the presence of such grandeur."

They laughed heartily. Trying to figure it out was probably the funniest thing a human being could do, and they laughed at themselves and the rest of humanity, trying to deal with the burden of living.

"You know Sam –"

They laughed again. "Now you're starting to do it." They were tired and giddy. The coffee was wearing off. When they finally settled down, Sam asked, "What were you going to say Edie?"

"Oh God, does it really matter?"

"Sure, go ahead."

"I learned another good saying in Spain this summer." As she had done previously when recalling her Spanish experience, she gathered her thoughts and tried to pronounce correctly. *"Los tontos lo pasan mejor.* Literally it means 'the fools pass it better'; it's their way of saying ignorance is bliss."

"Something like," our boy knit his brow as he searched for the correct phrase, "turn on the TV, watch pro wrestling, have a beer, and leave the driving to us. Right?"

"Hey," Edie blurted out, vaguely remembering some newscast or blurb, "isn't this guy Rodman a wrestler too?"

"Not exactly. I think he makes like –cameo appearances with pro wrestlers."

With their brains working overtime, our pair felt the need to relax, to settle down, to recharge a bit. They stared into space, scanning the impressive skyscape of inter-galactic beauty, consciously looking for more shooting stars, thus breaking one of the Holy Laws of the Universe, to wit: you will never see a shooting star if you are looking for one. After a few moments of fruitless vigilance, Edie returned to the task at hand.

"So what about this Rodman thing?"

Sam loved the intellectual perseverance of this woman. She was such a contrast to the usual cast of "fools passing it well." She stimulated him in every way. Unlike almost all the women he had dealt with in his life – and men too, who was he kidding – there was no need for busy talk or polite chatter. The awkward silence never lasted long with her. He could do something he had always longed for with a woman: he could really talk. It would truly be a shame if they could not consummate this thing.

"Dennis Rodman might be the first person to openly combine the sexual confusion of contemporary life – the muddling of the male-female roles, the unrest with monogamy and fidelity, etc. – with the macho aggression so glorified in our culture. It's not a pretty sight."

They sat silently once again, but this time the spectacular nocturnal show all around them was not part of the equation. It had now become habitual for them to mull over what had just been said. For these two, passing it well foolishly was not an option.

"Gosh Sam, I'd hate to think Dennis Rodman is where we are going."

"Look," said Sam, her words having snapped him out of his own inner thoughts, "let's not get too dramatic here. Rodman is the extreme case, the exaggeration of the idea. But even in its more moderate manifestations, it is not a good model to follow. That gets me back to my earlier point on what women are up to these days."

Edie shook her head and frowned. Once again, he had touched that live wire. The battle had been engaged one more time. It was a battle that lived close to the surface and any careless insinuation easily resumed the hostilities. "OK Sam," she challenged aggressively, "what about women?"

Her belligerence somewhat disappointed our man. He again thought he might be overrating her. Maybe she wasn't worth all this? He looked at her as she stared blindly out to sea. Oh God, he thought, he had to have her. He decided to gamble it all.

"Hey Edie –" he muttered as he began rummaging around in his pocket. He felt the same nervous tingle he had felt centuries ago on the Blanco Street Pier when he had first spoken to her; only now it was more than a tingle –it was almost a cold sweat. "– maybe you should just get on back." He pulled some coins from his pocket. "Here, maybe you should get yourself a cab."

Chapter 5

Extra Innings

What our pair was then experiencing went far beyond the dreaded awkward silence we have talked about all through this adventure. This was a full-blown crisis. The darkened atmosphere was charged with an inkiness that could almost be touched, as if the night all around them was beginning to melt, to become liquid, to become something that left an oily residue on their skin.

Ironically, in spite of the serious nature of the moment, the awkward silence is really a more negative thing than the heavy-handed angst experienced on that bench at the end of the world. The awkward silence as a chronic symptom is a form of indifference not worth rescuing; it is passionless, insipid, uncreative. It lacks the electricity and drama Sam and Edie had gone through at the current moment in this story. The charged atmosphere created when Sam pulled out those coins and suggested that Edie return alone was tangible proof their "relationship" was worth fighting for. Passionate struggle was certainly more worthwhile than laconic indifference.

Edie turned and kissed him chastely on the lips. Sam tried to escalate her advance, insinuating his tongue – but she quickly pulled away. He felt a mixture of relief – she had not taken him up on his offer – and disappointment. He slumped wearily on the bench.

Edie leaned back as well, rubbing her eyes methodically with her knuckles. She sighed heavily. "I'm sorry Sam, I'm such an idiot. Believe me, this is my problem, not yours."

"Easy for you to say."

The crisis had passed, but had anything been resolved? Sam tried to be positive. He had given her the chance to disengage, to get out of Dodge, but she was still there at his side. The night pressed in around them. The squawk of an unseen gull overhead punctuated the invisible silence. It would have been nice to have some more coffee.

"Edie," he spoke wearily, "could I have an update on where this game currently is?"

She didn't hesitate. "Extra innings." She laughed morbidly and continued. "It's a classic battle worthy of the history books."

"That depends on how it ends," he said dryly.

Edie nodded silently in sad recognition of the statement's truth. She decided to change the subject. "Sam, what is it you were wanting to tell me about women?"

It was after 2 o'clock in the morning.

Chapter 6

Macho Jerks

Sam realized he was still holding the coins in his hand. He stuffed them back in his pocket and sat up straight on the bench in an attempt to appease his cantankerous back. Perhaps under normal circumstances he would have stood up and stretched, but he feared that might signify something more serious, as if he were still in a crisis mode and wanted to bring this all to a head. In truth, that is exactly what he wanted to do; it's what he had wanted to do since he first saw her walking up the Blanco Street Pier – gosh, he thought to himself, was it really *yesterday* afternoon!

His mind felt rusted and over used. Did he really want to fall back into that limbo world they had been operating in, as if nothing had happened? Did he really want to discuss his theories on modern women? Who the hell cared? There was only one thing on his mind and he was kicking himself for being such a limp-dick, brain-fucked loser. He felt like a nerd.

"I'd really like to know," she repeated, "what you think about women these days."

And she really did want to know. Sam could feel her sincerity. It jarred him out of his self-pitying funk. This whole evening was beginning to drive him crazy, but it sometimes felt like a delicious kind of madness. He was sitting here in this beautiful place, under the stars, wooing a magnificent female creature he really had a shot at. Don't force it, he thought to himself. Don Juan has never been your thing. You are not Michael Jordan; let the game come to you.

He was beginning to feel schizophrenic; a moment ago he'd felt as if his pursuit of this girl had taken on epic proportions, as if he were Christopher Columbus desperately searching for a landfall he would never find. Now, just a few minutes later, he felt as if they had just begun, that it was only the first day. He told himself that time really wasn't the measure of his anxiety. If she were to tell him exactly one year from this day she would definitely let him have her, he'd be the happiest, most relaxed man in the world. Time had nothing to do with it, he told himself, relax, there's plenty of time.

If only he could believe it.

"You're not going to tell me?" she insisted.

Once again, the sound of her voice brought him to his senses. Lighten up, he thought, the Gillette Gods are dropping bombs on people in – where now? Some "Slabolastan" somewhere? What do you have to complain about, sitting here with this lovely woman?

"Oh God," he said sadly, "you really don't have to know, even if I could explain it."

Another car swung around the bend from the opposite direction and shined its lights directly on them. Its momentary intrusion seemed to put a hold on something, as if the page had been turned and a new chapter begun. When the light had passed, Sam asked, "You really want to hear what I have to say about women?"

Edie rolled her eyes and spoke sarcastically. "No, I only talk because I have a mouth."

"OK, but you have to promise not to get mad."

"I promise nothing."

Sam nodded and smiled. Once again, he was reminded his desire for her was not premised upon her being "a fool who passed it well."

"So?" The battle was about to culminate.

"Look Edie, it's not that women don't want to be housewives anymore that bothers me. What bothers me is what they want to be in its place. We've both agreed that traditional male behavior is perhaps a more guilty element in our society than the traditional female role – all the alley cat posturing and fighting, all the competition, all the 'I'm the man' machismo and chest thumping." He paused for a moment and took a deep breath, trying to gather his courage. "Are you with me so far?"

"Yeah, so far."

"OK, but here is the hard part. It seems that your solution to the problem, your way of getting out of the kitchen, is to be just like men; to be ass kicking athletes, ruthless business women, Machiavellian politicians and power lunch ogres. You should be demanding a softening male role, not a hardening female role. It's bad enough that men act like men, now you guys want it too. I want more ballet dancers who aren't fags as opposed to more dike-like basketball players. What are you trying to do; bring on Armageddon?" Fuck it, he thought, let's let it all hang out. ""I'm tired of men taking all the blame. I've been a gentleman all my life and you know what I've found out?" Edie stared mutely out to sea, refusing to look at him. "I've found out that most of you don't find that very sexy. Most of you go for the macho jerks. It's time to start looking in the mirror."

One might think that silence is something like being dead –you can't be more dead than dead. But there *are* different grades of silence. The silence left by Sam's harangue was as deep a silence as silence can be. Edie sat buried in that silence. She felt as if her mother had just scolded her.

From back across the beach road the far off sound of another off beat rooster – it was still way too early for the usual bantam serenade – let go a lusty call, like a dagger in the night. Just a generation or so ago, almost all the chickens in South Isle were owned and raised by someone, but the modern world of market research tourism had ended all that. Remarkably, the island's chicken population had thrived in the "wild." They could be seen and heard everywhere and had even become a tourist attraction. Now they were even out there by the airport, living blissfully in the mangroves. Edie had often thought they were the luckiest chickens in the world, free from factory farms and even domestication, living the chicken life on their own terms. How easy it was to be a chicken, she thought, as she struggled with the burden of being a human being.

"With this in mind," Sam went on in a timid attempt to save a perhaps already lost battle, "and in an effort to avoid a future world full of Dennis Rodmans, I make myself available as the first male participant in the grand old game of girl's basketball. It seems to be as fine a sport as any other sport. I see no reason for this game to die."

Edie had a determined look on her face as she got up and headed for the telephone.

Chapter 7

The Air We Breathe

*N*owadays we hear a lot about the "information age." Vast amounts of data can be stored in microscopic spaces. Judging from the slush we hear from the realm of Bill Gates, it seems that everything mankind has learned since the dawn of time –which probably means so much and so little at the same time –can now be stored in the brain of a hummingbird.

It took the taxi about 7 or 8 minutes to arrive. Sam continued to sit on the bench, gazing blankly out towards the South Pole. In an ominous display of indifference, Edie did not bother to join him. She stood by the phone and scanned the road, a taxi sentinel in the lonely night.

For the 7 or 8 minutes it took for that cab to arrive, Sam's brain turned into the natural version of those space age microchips that make a Pentagon full of file cabinets obsolete. It seemed as if his more than half century of life had been compressed into that 7 or 8 minute space. The myriad of things that passed through his mind as he blindly looked into the nothingness of the nocturnal ocean seemed too large for a microchip to hold. He remembered the home run he had hit in the Little League when he was 8 years old. He remembered having the mumps. He remembered the outrageous surprise when he jerked off for the first time in the shower. He remembered so many of the trivial triumphs and defeats of life, things that were taken so seriously at a certain point that turn out to be insignificant later on. He remembered being 10 years old and vowing to hate his mother eternally because she wouldn't let him have an ice cream bar too close to dinner. He remembered not talking to his dad for days because he wouldn't stay for the last 5 innings of a doubleheader at Yankee Stadium. He thought how inconsiderate and mean kids could be. And then there were the things that seemed unimportant at first that may have turned out to be transcendent in the end: books by Kurt Vonnegut or John Barth, movies like Dr. Strangelove and Putney Swope, smoking marijuana, but not for its mild physical effects, but more for the absurd hysteria the straight world lavished upon it. And then there were women! My God, did he ever remember women; women who wanted him but didn't turn him on (so many of them), women he wanted who wouldn't let him have them (so many more of those), and, most of all, he remembered the whole gamut of his modest stable of erotic triumph. The places he had done "it": in cars, in houses and apartments, in swimming pools, along the Blue Ridge Highway and in the Maritime Alps. And not just Americans but a whole atlas full of sexual goodwill and harmony: an Italian, various Brits, a Dane, a Canadian, more than one German, a Mexican, even a wonderful Chinese girl from Shanghai. He realized he had never had a red head. There was a black girl, a nurse, with Nubian breasts. And he even remembered the name of the girl who left him for Jesus. Tracy! And the first girl he'd ever lived with in South Isle, the blond bombshell, the incredible Fay. How could he have ever grown tired of that? And the places he had been: from Alaska to Bolivia, from Crete to Hawaii – and so many places in between. And everywhere he went – women! He realized how the sexual urge was the only urge, that all else would wither and turn to dust without its fertile pollination; no music, no sports, no literature, no poetry, no wars and politics, no Hitlers, Stalins and Clinton-Bushes, no video games, Lady Gaga or the crassness of the Super Bowl, without a stiff dick in search of a moist hole.

But a microchip is different from the human mind in some very essential ways. A microchip does not have a soul. It has no feelings. It is indifferent. It can never feel good or bad, happy or sad. Unlike the daunting couple of our story, it has no passions to be satisfied. It is not searching for such illusive, perhaps even trivial states of being such as "happiness." Even a eunuch has more passion than a microchip.

What Sam was feeling, above all else, for that 7 or 8 minutes, was something no microchip could ever feel: defeat and humiliation. His prospects with Edie seemed to be fading. Why didn't she come back and sit with him? He was on the verge of feeling depressed. Edie and her sermon on such be damned, he was feeling depressed. The kaleidoscope of his life passing before him was not a fond remembrance. His imminent failure with this girl he had emotionally invested so much in had soured his mood and made his life seem like it didn't need to have happened. So much time, so many places, so many things experienced and done – and what? He was not young anymore. It all suddenly seemed like a big waste of time. He was reminded of something Edie had said earlier – what was it? Something about this supposedly being the happiest society in the history of mankind – something about it being hard to live up to that standard?

He felt tired.

"C'mon Sam." Her voice startled him. He turned and saw her standing by the side of the cab, holding the door for him. She wasn't going to leave him there. He felt rejuvenated, reborn. There was still hope. That's all there ever was and ever will be, thought Sam, as he got up and headed towards the open door. Hope! It was the air we breathed.

Chapter 8

Utah, 1864

*C*ontrary to the 7 or 8 minutes of desperation experienced by Sam on that seaside bench, Edie had stood by the phone in a state of total serenity. She had come to a decision; she knew exactly how all of this would end.

When Sam got in the car Edie closed the door behind him. For a brief instance in eternity, he felt panic as he realized she might be sending him back without her. But she walked behind the rear of the vehicle and entered from the other side. She had already told the driver to go back to town the long way, around the eastern tip of the island, increasing the journey by about 10 minutes. She wanted to prolong it a bit. She knew how important it would be.

As we all know by now, the fair lady of our story was not a bad human being. She was not a sadist. She didn't want to hurt anyone, least of all this wonderful man she seemed to have devoted a lifetime to in less than one day. As she had watched him by the phone for that 7 or 8 minutes of history, she could feel his anguish. But she was also human. She had her pride. She could feel the power of her feminine allure and it made her feel alive, like living this life had suddenly become all worthwhile. She marveled at the fact that she could bring on such feelings in another human being. She realized she was playing with him at that moment, like a cat teasing a lizard, something she could give herself the luxury to do because she knew what would happen next.

Picture yourself, dear reader, at a baseball game. It is the bottom of the 9th – no, by now, as we all know, we have gone into extra innings. The visitors have scored a run in the top half of the inning and lead 3 to 2. There are 2 outs for the home team and there is a runner on first. There are 2 strikes on the batter, a big burly clean up hitter. The pitcher whirls and delivers and the big stud swings mightily. There is a clean crack as the wooden bat explodes its fury upon the horsehide ball. Almost immediately, long before the ball has flown its majestic arc to the distant stands beyond the beautifully manicured field, before it has even left the infield, a sudden charge of electric ecstasy bolts through the home crowd. Marlins win! Marlins win!

This is how Sam felt when Edie opened the door on the opposite side of the taxi and slid all the way over to his side of the seat, thigh tightly pressed to thigh, like high school sweethearts at the drive-in. The space on the empty two thirds of the seat seemed to convey an immense message. He put his arm around her and she snuggled closer, resting her head on his shoulder. A minute later, as they passed the community of houseboats clinging to shore in the Hog Island Channel, they were passionately kissing each other, their tongues having finally met after so much effort. For an absurd moment – and for reasons so absurd they could never be explained – Sam thought of the historic meeting of the rail lines in Utah in 1864.

The cabbie smiled as he briefly viewed the scene in his rear view mirror. For him, this was routine stuff. He'd seen it a thousand times. For a third person viewing 2 lovers – holding hands as they walked along, kissing on a blanket at the beach, or sitting close in a taxi in the wee hours of the morning – it always seemed so routine. For the rest of humanity, what 2 lovers are doing seems to be the most routine thing in the world. But for the 2 lovers themselves, it is the only thing *not* routine in their whole lives.

How to keep it from becoming routine was the $64 question.

Chapter 9

Patriotism

Although it was not the first time they had seen or spoken to each other, Sam and Edie had really begun to know each other about 10 hours before. For almost half a day they had done nothing but talk – and talk and talk. But the taxi ride had changed everything. Without having to actually perform the sexual act, they had already become lovers. The taxicab had become a shrine of sorts, a shrine that should not be profaned with talk. It had become a Holy Place.

For the 15 minutes it took to be deposited in front of the lane where Edie lived, not one word was spoken. That initial moment of passion as they passed the houseboats was the only kiss they exchanged during that memorable journey. They sat close, her head on his shoulder. He took in the lovely aroma of her satiny blond hair. They pressed close together, feeling the pulse of each other's body. They did not talk. There was no pressure to talk. They immersed themselves in the delicious experience of being alive.

But they were thinking, and some of the things they thought are worth recording.

For Sam, his impending triumph with this splendid woman seemed to have validated his whole life. He realized he always felt like this when he was successful with a woman worth the effort. Just a few moments before, he had felt like a total failure. He had felt as if his flight from the "old country"; that his bohemian escape from a white collar career had gotten him nowhere, sitting on a bench, alone and unfulfilled. He had outsmarted himself with his up yours attitude towards the Murdoch world of objective news swindling. And now, just 5 minutes later, he had turned abject defeat into glorious victory. He looked back on his life and thought he had done everything exactly right. He wouldn't have changed a thing.

Edie's thoughts were in a more practical realm. It had been so long since she had desired a man it was beginning to worry her. The pride and power she felt in her sexual allure was a re-encounter with herself. She had a right to such a birthright as a woman. She had begun to think she had lost it. She now realized she could not feel such power if there was no one she wanted to use it upon. It was something like being a good cricket player in a country where nobody knew anything about cricket. She snuggled closer to her man. She could feel the increased pace of his heartbeat. She felt the exhilaration of diving into an aqua colored pool on a hot day. She felt good.

The cab passed through the light where the road leading off the island and back to the rest of the world turned to the right. They went straight ahead and around the bend which headed back to town on the island's biggest thoroughfare, a four-lane artery known as Monroe Avenue. The "Avenue," as it was known locally, was the essence of the New Barrio. Except for the palm trees that stood in place of the rest of the country's more temperate vegetation, this was one stencil America in all its horror, a fast food wasteland of shopping malls and used car lots, a neon desert of lead free fuel and Walgreen's-Blockbuster predictability, a wonder world of Nike-Reebok polyester for the Third World mentality.

The cab began to slow as it approached a red light at a big intersection. One of the corners was occupied by a cheaper but still expensive motel (all lodging was expensive on the island), the South Isle. The o and the u on the pink neon sign were not working, leaving an uneven hieroglyphic for the weary traveler to read. A Kenny Rogers chicken joint stood on another corner. The darkened façade of its non-business hours were more than made up for by the screeching naked light of a 24-hour convenience store doing business across the street. A baseball field slumbering for the winter completed the topography of this typical American landscape.

The cab found itself coasting to a stop behind a big garbage truck, out and about on the flip side of life that is waste disposal. Like a contented lion that had just completed a good meal, the opening where the garbage disappeared into the big truck's innards yawned wide open before them. The whole scene, in some kind of mysterious chemical reaction, triggered Sam's memory and made him think of a moment in his life that had been somewhat of an epiphany for him. He would tell Edie about it later that morning, as they sat contentedly in her comfortable home.

For the first few years after he had ripped off his tie and stuffed it into his pocket for good, Sam had continued to live in the "grimy urban disaster," keeping himself alive with a varying array of proletarian jobs. One of them had been delivering auto parts around the metropolitan area of a city that shall go unnamed, all such places being sufficiently similar to render such information irrelevant.

In any event, this job put our boy in contact with the more Big League versions of Monroe Avenue on a daily basis; six- and eight-lane extravaganzas timed to the constant rhythms of green, yellow and red, horizon bound for as far as the eye could see. Like the endless banana cultivations he had seen in Nicaragua, the concrete plantations of American consumerism seemed to go on forever – the "drive thru" world of Big Macs and ATM money, from the credit card domain of Bloomingdale's to the K-Mart schlock of immigrant dreams.

As Sam sat in that taxi on Monroe Avenue, he could not help but think of one particular day spent delivering auto parts. It was late winter, cold and raw, and a light rain had fallen all day, exaggerating the usual gloom this urban landscape had begun to cause in him. The traffic, hindered by the bad conditions, was more horrendous than usual and he was running late. He was falling into a weary funk as the end of his workday seemed to stretch as interminably before him as the never-ending vista of parking lots and shopping centers. As the light he approached turned from yellow to red he found himself gliding to a stop behind a huge white garbage truck. He ground to a halt and numbly began to scan the world around him.

Sam pulled Edie closer as he marveled at the clarity of his memory. As we shall find out a bit further on, Edie was thinking her own thoughts as she snuggled deliciously tighter.

Sam remembered it as if it were happening in the present tense. As he sat sullenly behind that garbage truck so long ago, he had begun singing what he had long decided was perhaps the most relevant song ever written in the industrial era – **you pave paradise, put up a parking lot**. Thirty some odd years later, and more than a thousand miles from that disastrous intersection back in the "old country," he felt the song more relevant than ever. Yes, Joni, I hear you girl.

The light turned green before our couple's taxi and the garbage truck arthritically lurched into motion. As the trip back to the Old Barrio continued, the trip back in time continued in Sam's memory. The movement of that big white garbage truck back in Sam's biography – Moby Garbage Truck, he remembered thinking at the time –had snapped him back to reality. As he peered forward and concentrated on his driving, it seemed as if he could accelerate and drive right up into Moby's belly, right into its hippo mouth through which the excrement of our industrial assholes passed daily. And then he saw it! Painted on Moby's rear end was an American flag with the words "be proud for what it stands for" printed under it. At first he thought this was a strange place for such patriotic exhortation, but then, like a religious revelation, he suddenly realized how appropriate it was. What could be more synonymous with America than garbage? Undoubtedly, a decrease in garbage would not bode well for the economy. A healthy American economy demands more garbage. What better place to express your love for America than on a garbage truck?

Two weeks later he had left the "old country" and begun his pilgrimage, which eventually led him to the end of the road – South Isle.

Chapter 10

A Friend for Life

*W*hile Sam was reminiscing about that fateful encounter with Moby Garbage Truck, Edie's mind had been in a country far, far away, revolving around in her own brewery of thoughts. Now that the pressure was off she felt relieved and comfortable with her decision. She felt so relaxed, with her head buried into his shoulder, her mind felt free to run in any direction.

While stopped at the light, the haphazard angle of her head pointed directly at the profanity of the convenience store on the corner. She noticed the price of gasoline shining brightly in the naked neon light. My God, it was 10 cents cheaper when she'd filled her 15-year-old Volkswagen just two days before. Oil, she thought, was the world's biggest scam. Some unseen, omnipotent skyscraper God waves his magic wand and – *presto!* – you will now pay whatever the Gillette Gods are demanding.

For some reason or other, this all made her think of Sam's bicycle thief parody of "What's My Line?" She suddenly realized how profound he had been with that piece, that being a thief was really just a matter of perception.

She found herself admiring him even more as she burrowed deeper into his sinewy masculine shoulder. How did she put it –? "Some gets bought, some gets stolen, some gets insured" – Insurance! Boy, there's another one. Exxon, Allstate – talk about legal rackets. This was the "legal underworld" in all its glory. Or maybe it should be known as the "Protestant Mafia," or –

The self-serving interests of real power, she reasoned, always try to sanitize themselves behind distorting veils of respectability. But when the cows are finally brought in for the night, what did our society really stand for? It certainly provided fertile ground for stealing. If you stole a little they called you a thief. If you stole a lot – and the more the better – they put you on the Nasdaq and called you a modern day hero.

The light changed and the cab started forward. The price of gas retreated into the night. Edie wondered how she had gotten started on that. Bitch, bitch, bitch. Sure, she thought, why not? Now that she felt like a woman again, now that she was on her way home with a man she wanted, now that she had a feeling others wanted, she could bitch to her hearts content. The mopey Edie that had wandered out to the Blanco Street Pier that afternoon had no such right. That Edie was not at peace with herself. That Edie had no right to preach to anyone.

Ten minutes later the cab sped off into the underbelly of the wee hours, leaving our pair standing at the top of the lane where Edie lived. It felt good to be back in the Old Barrio, as if they had just gotten home from a long trip. The wooden homes peeking out from behind the dense tropical foliage seemed to fit just right, like an old baseball glove that had been broken in perfectly.

They stood under a huge mahogany tree. The dim beige light from the streetlight above sifted its way through the movement of the leaves in the cool northern air, creating a twinkling effect on the ground. When they made eye contact, their lips instinctively sought fleshy contact. They deliciously nibbled at each other until their tongues came together once again. Upon breaking apart, they immediately melted into a warm embrace.

A few moments later they were walking down the lane towards Edie's little cottage. The lane was barely wide enough for a car to pass through, something which only happened for the most essential purposes. The thick growth of bougainvilleas, aurelias, Surinam cherry bushes, and a whole host of trees and vines, further impinged upon the lane's original width, making it more like a footpath than a street. The cottage stood at the end of the dead end lane.

About half way down the lane the accelerated clicking of a small dog approaching burst into their consciousness. They soon saw a small Chihuahua mutt with ears too big for his body come flying out of the darkness. When he had arrived, he braked recklessly and began jumping up and down on Edie's legs, like a cocaine marionette bursting out of its own energy.

She bent down and calmed the dog, who let loose with a tandem of shrill little dog yips and yaps. Soon he was slopping her face with wet doggy kisses.

"OK, OK," she talked calmly, soothingly, "that's right, I'm home, I'm home – that's a good boy." She stroked his head, his snout, his silly Dumbo ears. "That's a good boy." When she had completely calmed him, she stood up and began fumbling in her waist purse. The dog noticed Sam and began to size him up, sniffing his pants cuff as if he were seeing through his nose. He was hesitant but not hostile.

Edie pulled out the Slim Jim she had bought back at the Cuban grocery store. As she pulled off the wrapper she introduced the two men. "Sam, I'd like you to meet Pancho. Pancho, Sam." She then handed Sam the doggy treat and motioned with her head for him to give it to the dog. Sam bent down and handed Pancho his snack. The little dog snatched it greedily and devoured it in short order. He then turned back to Sam and began planting the same sloppy kisses on his face that he had painted Edie with moments before. They were now friends for life.

Sam stood up and the three of them headed down the lane together. The rapid clicks of the dog's paws on the broken pavement led the way. Sam noticed the door was unlocked as Edie swung it open and clicked on a reddish-colored light.

Chapter 11

The Olduvai Gorge

*E*die had lived in South Isle for more than 20 years. She was a veteran. She knew what she wanted from a place to live and knew how to go about it. She had found this place five years ago and was sure it had a lot to do with her still being on the island.

The reader might remember an anecdote from this story where a girl friend of our heroine came to her and complained of being "depressed." Her boy friend had left her, what to do, etc. and blah, blah. Edie, as she explained to Sam way back when, had had very little patience with it all, etc. and blah, blah. This girl, along with her then boyfriend, had been the previous occupants of the cottage. After they split, she had decided to go back to the "old country" in pursuit of some career opportunity. She had decided to go back and "join up." She was nice enough to give Edie dibs on the house.

When Edie was given the opportunity she asked her friend if she could have three or four days to decide. She found out the owner of the cottage was a Leno woman of about 55 years who lived in the big house next door. She was a widow and shared her house with her daughter and son in law, along with their two young kids. The big house and the cottage, which had been built 75 years ago to house a single relative in the family's extensive genealogy, had been in the family for generations. Edie's first objective had been met: the house would not be sold out from under her.

For the next four days she would come snooping around at all different times of day. She was testing the noise level; were there party types with invasive musical armaments? Were there televisions infecting the air with canned laughter and shoot-'em up hooting and hollering? She knew she'd be working in her house and had great sensitivities for such things.

In the end, it had turned out to be perfect. The lane was a beautiful hideaway and almost all it residents were non-transient veterans. They loved the lane and wanted to maintain its serenity. This was Old Barrio living at its finest.

Upon entering the cottage, Edie pointed Sam towards a worn out sofa fronted by an old coffee table. She and Pancho headed for a cozy kitchen that formed part of the main room at its far end. A counter with some stools in front of it separated the kitchen from the living area.

As Sam plopped down on the comfortable sofa, Edie put some water on to boil. "How 'bout some tea?"

"Perfect."

"Do you like peppermint?"

"Perfect."

She laid out two cups on a tray, placing the tea bags next to them. She then took out a can of dog food from under the sink and slid it into Pancho's bowl on the kitchen floor. Such was the little dog's joy that he stood on his hind legs and pranced before her like a diminutive circus bear. The sounds of his gluttonous attack on his meaty feast could soon be heard in the whole house.

With the water heating up and the dog lustily pursuing

his culinary passions, Edie took off the jacket Sam had lent her and adjourned to a room that had to be the bedroom. He could dimly hear her checking the messages she'd received on her iPhone as he began scanning his lover's house. Although the furnishings seemed to be no more than a varying array of yard sale castaways, there was an elegance to the place that could not be overlooked. All the little niceties of life – the knick-knacks and cushions, the upholstery, the pictures on the walls, the place settings and coasters for glasses – seemed to be of a similar style. It was a colorful, tropical motif of exotic birds and flowers, flowering trees and wind blown palms, banana plants and tropical fruits – mangos, papayas, sugar apples and guavas.

Remarkably enough, he noticed as he took it all in, except for the elegance and taste that could not be bought at any price, there was virtually nothing of value here. Except for a radio sitting on the counter in front of the kitchen and a small television staring at him from across the room, the usual line up of electronic gadgetry now deemed necessary for the modern concept of happiness, was totally absent.

He could now see why she, like him, never locked her door. Stealing on South Isle, as in other parts of the realm, was a well-developed art form. But stealing was really just a function of materialism. The more people were led into needing things, the more stealing there would be. He remembered Edie's cogent remarks on "not needing." Except for the elegance displayed in this house, he realized his place was quite similar. What was there to steal?

Sitting there in that lovely home on the verge of such a wonderful romantic triumph, Sam had felt more optimistic than usual. Perhaps people like himself and Edie were in the vanguard of a new kind of human being. Yes, he thought, perhaps they represented the next stage in the evolution of man: from the cave dwellers of the Olduvai Gorge up through the history of the species – drum roll, please – to **Post Consumer Man**.

Such grandiose thoughts were suddenly broken when a magnificent male cat leisurely strolled through the front door. His coal black coat shined dramatically in the dim light as he gracefully crossed the room. He had a relaxed, athletic stride reminiscent of the great baseball player, Henry Aaron. His regal bearing gave the impression that he owned the place.

About half way across the room he noticed Sam on the sofa. He stopped and examined him at length with his laser-like emerald eyes. There was no fear, no hostility, no warmth and no surprise. When he was satisfied this insignificant part of the world around him posed no threat, he continued his leisurely stroll across the room, finishing his journey with an effortless leap onto the counter in front of the kitchen. He landed lightly on the Formica top, rolled himself into a black lump of fur, and began dozing peacefully.

Our man, who just a second ago was feeling as if he were breaking new evolutionary ground, felt humbled in the presence of such self confident beauty.

Chapter 12

The NFL

"Hey," said Sam, trying to get Edie's attention, "who's this?"

Her head appeared in the bedroom doorway. "Who?"

He pointed at the ebony Rajah. "Him."

"Oh, him." She seemed to have mixed feelings. "That's Buster Black."

The water kettle began to whistle. Edie hurried over and shut off the stove. She opened a cupboard and took out a box of cookies which she deposited on the tray with the porcelain cups. Both the cups and tray were artistically festooned with the beautiful design of a colorful parrot. A few seconds later she had placed it all on the table before the sofa and sat down next to her loving guest. They looked at each other, smiled, kissed briefly, and turned to their late night snack.

"Wow!" said Sam, "Those minty little Girl Scout cookies. I love them."

"I'm not exactly a big fan of the Girl Scouts," replied Edie, as she poured the steaming water into the cups, "but anyone who doesn't like these cookies should be examined by modern science."

"Or stalked by the CIA."

They laughed as they began to enjoy their elegant nightcap snack. The hot tea went down perfectly in the cool night air and the cookies appeased a hunger that had bubbled to the surface as the tension of the night's amorous struggle had been broken. For a few minutes they snacked in silence until Sam came up for air. He was not quite finished with the cookie he was chewing when he pastily asked, "So tell me about the cat." He immediately washed it down with a sip of tea.

Edie swallowed a delicate piece of the sweet, minty dessert. "Buster Black showed up here about 2 years after I'd moved in. I'd been living with a guy for almost that whole time and it had begun to get old – if you know what I mean."

"No need to explain."

"Anyway, that's when His Royal Highness showed up." She motioned with her head to where the feline beauty was supposedly napping. He could feel he was somehow part of the conversation and one of his piercing green eyes cracked open in a slit of recognition. "He charmed me right from the start. He was gaunt and almost scrawny and his fight to survive was entering a critical stage, and yet, with his pleading eyes and beseeching meows he was an imposing personality. He would come in and playfully swat at my feet, and rub up against me. I wasn't really up for having a cat, but he kept coming around and getting bolder. He would jump into my lap and press his head against my forehead and meow, meow." She bent forward and grabbed her teacup, washing down the stickiness caused by her story telling. "Like I was saying, he was so cute. It was like having George Clooney falling in love with you. But after a month or so, once he had solidified his place in the household, cute turned into indifference. Buster Black is a shrewd operator, believe me."

Sam turned and looked at the subject of the

252

conversation. By now he had lost interest in his own celebrity and had turned his back on them, curling into a tighter ball of fur, getting serious about his late night nap. An audible sigh could be heard as he buried his head under one of his paws.

"But Buster Black," she went on, "in his own selfish way, pointed me where I had to go." She put down the cup and reached for another cookie. Before biting into it, she began to explain. "There I was, living with 2 men with the same attitude. In truth, the thrill had worn off for Jeff – that was my boyfriend – a good year before we finally broke up. But he liked the house, he liked the life, and he could still service me once in awhile if he got stoned enough. After awhile I was getting pretty fed up playing second fiddle to the NFL." She stopped and inserted the cookie into her mouth. She ate the whole thing, like a pelican gulping down a complete fish and followed it with a hearty swig of tea. "When Buster began to treat me the same way as Jeff, something in me snapped. Up until then, I was too timid – " she shook her head. "No, that really wasn't it. Basically, I was too lazy to break the routine, to start anew, to dive into the unknown once again. But when Buster Black started to piss me off, I became a time bomb ready to go off. One afternoon I walked into the house and found Jeff in his usual spot in front of the TV. I went right for the set and shut it off. 'Hey', he said, 'it's the fourth quarter.' 'You better believe it,' I replied, 'this game is almost over.' I gave him 24 hours to get out. I've had a few other affairs since, but nobody has ever lived here with me again. I don't let stale love affairs linger anymore. I –"

She realized this conversation was making Sam

uncomfortable. She leaned over and kissed him on the cheek. "Hey, big boy, tonight is another day."

Sam motioned with his eyes towards the kitchen counter. "How come he's still here?"

She smiled and shook her head in sad resignation. "There's no getting rid of Buster. At least he's a good mouser."

"Well, I warn you, I'm not much of a mouser, but you're not getting rid of me so easy either."

They kissed deeply. When they parted, Edie pointed towards the bedroom. "Go, go," she said, as she shooed him away. "I'll meet you in there." When he had disappeared inside the bedroom door she gathered the cookies, the teacups, and the whole fandango and deposited it all in the sink, running enough water over everything to keep the ants off. Pancho had fallen asleep beside his empty bowl. She picked it up and put it in the sink as well. She flicked off the light in the room and headed for the bedroom, leaving Buster Black in deep slumber doing what he always did: whatever he wanted.

The front door was left slightly open.

Chapter 13

Fuck'em

$\mathcal{S}$omewhere around nine the next morning, a ray of sun managed to sift and work its way through the foliage outside the window where Sam and Edie were contentedly sleeping as only 2 satisfied lovers could. With the tireless persistence that light possesses, it found a crack in the venetian blind and made its way in a thread-like slither to the corner of our boy's right eye. He blinked foggily for a couple of seconds and realized he was awake. He looked to his left and saw the beautiful woman who had made life worthwhile once again, curled in a fetal position facing away from him under the blanket, a blanket with a colorful coconut palm bending across its length. He examined her as only a newfound lover could. He could not see her face but knew she was sleeping peacefully, unhindered by any emotional struggles brought on by the human condition.

He breathed deeply, smiled, and put his hands behind his head. As he gazed up at the ceiling, he began thinking about the wonderful moments they had passed together just a few hours before. He reveled in what was perhaps the greatest moment a man could live: the moment when a first time lover whose erotic side had still not been seen, who perhaps had seemed even chaste until that moment, let down all her defenses and, like the most liberated – or depraved – porno star, let loose all her passionate impulses in a way not even imagined until then. At times, what a man fantasizes about a still untested woman turns out to be better than the real thing – and then there are those other times when the imagination falls short of reality.

By the time she had entered the room, Sam remembered, he was already undressed and under the light blanket. She closed the door gently behind her, leaving an impenetrable darkness that momentarily disappointed him until she flipped on a small lamp on a dresser beside the door. The lampshade shielded the light from the little bulb, throwing off a fuzzy, orangey glow. She immediately began taking off her clothes. There were no flirtatious affectations or strip tease. When she was completely naked, she stepped to the front of the bed and stood before him with her hands provocatively on her hips, as if to say, "What do you think?" Her breasts were larger than he thought they'd be and were generously crowned with the pale pink of the true blond. Her legs were wide apart and her light colored bush stood defiantly before him. His erection was so swift and so intense that the bulge in the blanket could not be overlooked. "Well, Sam," she had said with an impish smile, "I know you don't carry a gun so there is no need to ask the question, is there?" She pulled the blanket off and began to methodically work her way onto the anxious member, leaning forward a bit, letting her generous endowment sway rhythmically before him as she became wetter, moister, more ready for action. Sam began to caress the swinging ornaments –

As Sam lay in the sweet morning light of his lover's bed and thought back on the sexual fiesta they had just lived, unbeknownst to him his eyes began to close as he faded into an erotic dream. A finger was running smoothly along his dick which began to straighten and rise from its placid slumber. "Sam?" He heard the soft whisper and briefly opened his eyes. He was not dreaming. Edie had come out of her fetal sleep and lay face up on the pillow. She lay motionless except for the stroking of the object of her affections. "When you write your book, are you going to include all the good stuff, like what I'm doing to you right now?"

It really wasn't a propitious moment to be thinking about anything. He was just lucid enough to say, as he rolled over and began to mount the prize, "No, fuck'em."

Chapter 14

The Phone

*B*y 10 o'clock Sam found himself sitting on a stool on the living room side of the counter. Like the snack the night before, the breakfast was simple but elegant. The toast was a beautiful 7-grain bread made at a local bakery. The butter was a natural vegetable spread that could pass for Land o' the Lakes. A lovely raspberry preserve, from a picturesque farm in the Napa Valley, rounded out the solid part of the "*petit dejuener*." But the "*coup de grace*" was the liquid refreshment: a natural strawberry juice from the Finger Lakes region of New York State. It was cold and it was delicious.

Sam suddenly realized everything about this girl was simple but elegant.

"You know Edie –" they laughed as they realized he had just uttered his favorite line again. "Hey," he muttered while swallowing a hardy gulp of the exquisite juice, "that's the first time I've said it in hours."

"Yeah, but you were sleeping –"

"Or fucking."

They laughed a bit more as Edie bit into a piece of toast. She was standing on the kitchen side of the counter and had just laid out some food for Buster Black who was heartily doing away with his breakfast in the same place where Pancho ate. "What were you going to say?"

"Back when I was a more hormonally desperate young buck —"

"Oh," Edie cut in, "and you are not so desperate now?"

Sam put some jelly on another piece of toast. He smiled. "That depends more on the lady these days." Edie reached her hand across the counter and caressed his moneychanger's face. How deceiving looks can be, she thought. Sam grabbed the hand, kissed it and continued with what he was going to say. "Anyway, back then, when I was a young single fresh out of law school in the big city, me and a buddy of mine would rate our infrequent feminine conquests by the quality of the orange juice in the morning." He stopped and nibbled on some toast.

"Sorry, I used to drink tons of orange juice until I realized it sometimes upset my stomach. These softer juices —"

"No, no," he interrupted, "this is fantastic. If I had come across this back then I'd have probably married the girl."

"And lived unhappily ever after, deceived by a glass of strawberry juice."

Edie's iPhone began making the strange noises these devices make when someone is trying to get in touch. There was no musical selection, only the default noise from the factory. Edie took a swig of juice and adjourned to the bedroom, from where the strange alert was emanating. After a brief, muffled conversation, she returned to the kitchen counter. "Boy, sometimes I hate phones."

"I lived in South Isle for 25 years without a phone," said Sam, as he munched on his toast.

"My, my, but aren't we primitive. What did you do for hot food; rub 2 sticks together?"

He dusted off his piece of toast and took a long swallow of the rich red juice. He knew he wasn't the most conventional person in the world, but not having a phone was a bit beyond the pale. "I –" he shrugged, trying to find a good explanation. "Maybe it had to do with money. The first few years I lived in South Isle I was always living on the edge. A phone was just another expense. After awhile I got used to not having one." He reached for another piece of toast. "To be quite frank, whenever I hear a phone ring I'm happy to know it is not for me."

For the next few minutes they silently indulged themselves. Sam found Edie's telephone habit a bit out of character, like a suburban housewife with little to do but gossip and shop with the kids in school and the old man at work. He finished off another piece of toast – God, he was hungry – and wiped his mouth with a napkin taken from a wooden holder shaped like an egret. "I must admit Edie, it seems a little – I don't know – not you."

"Not me?"

"Yeah. All these phone calls and messages."

She threw her head back and smiled. "Ha! Business Sam, business."

"You own a business?"

She pondered the situation as she watched Buster Black quickly head for the front door, his morning meal completed. Contrary to his leisurely arrivals, he was always in a hurry to leave. "Yeah, I have a business. Just about everything you see here, the knick-knacks and accessories, were designed by me."

"Really?" He turned and scanned the room, taking in all the brightly colored ornaments and cushions and all the other things he could now recognize as the artistic work of one person.

"I have some buyers up north who are always nagging me for more stuff, haggling about prices – biness man, biness," she mimicked the speech of the black dude in those silly Jackie Chan movies. "Oh, I almost forgot."

She hurried into the bedroom and quickly returned with her waist purse. She opened it on the counter and took out the frangipane flower she had picked up the night before. "I've been thinking of making some pot holders and I thought a design like this, with these flowers, might be nice." She spread it before them on the counter. "What do you think?"

Sam shook his head and marveled at the talent of this woman. "Edie, the only thing that matters is what *you* think. Judging from this room, that's a sure bet."

The phone rang again.

Chapter 15

Tribal Mumbo Jumbo

As Edie occupied herself with the intervention of the 21st Century's communication devices, Sam continued eating. The staccato clicking of a small dog's advance suddenly insinuated itself into the mood of the relaxed morning. Our boy looked up and saw Pancho crossing the wood floor in his direction. He had probably seen the cat exit and had decided it was his turn now. Not being one to forget a hand out, he planted himself steadfastly next to one of Sam's legs and looked longingly up with his large Chihuahua eyes. His new friend broke off a piece of bread and placed it right in front of the dog's snout. Pancho sniffed it suspiciously and took it in his mouth. He chewed briefly and let the now soggy mass drop to the ground.

Edie came out of the bedroom smiling and shaking her head. The dog immediately noticed her presence and ran gleefully to where his clean dish laid waiting on the kitchen floor. As Edie picked up the cat's bowl and rinsed it in the sink, the canine part of her menagerie went into his circus act, standing comically on his hind legs. "OK, OK, take it easy."

"Hey, your dog's not a vegetarian." Sam leaned down and captured the rejected mouthful in a napkin.

As she bent over and placed his dish of dog food on the floor, she playfully spoke right to the dog's face. "He's a dog,

he's a hunter, a predator, a killer, meat, meat, *rrraarrr* –"
She grabbed a sponge and threw it to her companion who
plucked it deftly from the air with one hand. He wiped the
floor clean and gave it back to Edie who continued munching
on her side of the counter. "You better eat fast," said Sam
sarcastically, "that phone might go off any minute."

She shook her head and sipped some juice. "I know, I
know." She wondered if her business was starting to get too
big, to get out of hand. She certainly didn't want all that to
run her life, but it was like a monster that needed more food
all the time. She was finding out you couldn't tell people to
slow down, to take it easy, to mellow out. They always
wanted it now; they always wanted more – and you better
have it or they'd go somewhere else. A Frankenstein had
been created and she began to realize it wasn't just her – it
was the whole way in which we lived.

"Believe it or not, that last call was from my mother."

"Your mother?"

"Yeah." She smiled ambiguously and nibbled on some
more toast. Her silence was ambiguous as well.

"Do you have problems with your mother?"

She arched her eyebrows and gave it some thought. "No,
not really. We've never stopped being mother and daughter,
but it was very hard at first."

"At first?"

"Yeah – when I stopped being a political science major
and left it all behind."

Sam almost choked on the piece of toast he was chewing
on. He cleared his mouth with a gulp of juice and said, "tell
me about it! When I pulled off my tie for the last time my
parents freaked."

"When it became obvious that a husband and grandchildren were not a big part of the plan –" She stopped and gazed across the room, looking at nothing, conjuring up the past. "I remember writing my mom a letter back then gently saying she shouldn't be such an asshole, that everything was alright, don't worry. She promptly wrote back saying that I was being silly, it was time to be a grown up, I was not a girl anymore and that 'such language was not becoming of a young lady'. In my next letter to her I wrote, 'Dear Mom, I'm sorry for the savage way in which I used the language, but what the fuck'."

"Trying to raise mother can be quite a chore."

"Oh God, I finally began to realize not trying to raise her was the best policy." Pancho finished eating and the clickety-click of his little paws played like a salsa rhythm as he headed for the door. "But that was then. It took a while for her to realize I was not drugged, promiscuous and dying, and now we get along fine. But I know deep down that a husband and grandchildren are still what she wants."

"Normal," uttered Sam, as he wiped his mouth and stretched his body into a more relaxed state of being.

"Except for me, my family is a classic study in normalcy."

Sam blew some air out and shrugged his shoulders. "Oh, let's not give ourselves too much credit. A black sheep here and there is normal as well, don't you think? It's what makes the world go round."

Edie finished off her breakfast and began wiping down the counter before her, flipping the sponge in the sink behind her. Our pair retreated into their own thoughts as she picked up Pancho's bowl, washed it, and put it back under the sink. They were both pondering the mere idea of being alive and what it had all led to. Sam's family history had been very similar to Edie's and there was no need to expound upon it. "You know Edie," this time nobody cared about his usual refrain, "sometimes I think all this tribal mumbo-jumbo is at the core of everything gone wrong on this planet."

"Sam, would you like some coffee?"

Chapter 16

Early Wynn

*A*s Edie began to put the water on to boil, Sam gathered the dishes and the rest of the eating paraphernalia and brought it into the kitchen. "Where does the food go?" Edie pointed to a plastic lined garbage can next to the stove. He scraped the remains of their breakfast off the plates and began washing them in the sink. Edie laid out the cups and saucers on the same tray they had used the night before. When the coffee pot started to whistle, she deposited it on the tray, got a sugar bowl out of the cupboard along with some milk and headed to the sofa, putting the tray on the coffee table. She sat down and waited for her boy to finish cleaning.

A minute later Sam plopped down on the sofa next to her and she began pouring the coffee. They lightened and sweetened to their own tastes and finally took that delicious first sip.

"What was it you were saying about tribal mumbo-jumbo?" She leaned forward and added a bit more sugar.

Sam placed his cup back on the tray and began his discourse. "Last night, when you were in the bedroom checking all your phone messages, Buster Black strolled on in."

"I know. What's that got to do with tribal mumbo-jumbo?"

"Patience Edie, patience."

"Sorry. Sometimes I get a little hyper."

"Go easy on the coffee."

She brought the freshly sweetened brew to her lips, sipped daintily, and put the cup back on the tray. "Ah, just right."

"I wish we had more of those Girl Scout cookies."

"Well, if you hadn't gone through them like a famine survivor –"

"I think they should call those things heroine cookies. I just couldn't stop."

"I doubt if the Girl Scouts would go for that." She took another sip of the rich blend. "Tribal mumbo-jumbo?"

"Oh yeah. When the cat jumped up on the counter and began to sleep –he was so beautiful and so imposing I could not help but stare at him. Eventually, my vision came to rest on his stomach rhythmically moving up and down as he breathed. Up and down, in and out. Up and down, in and out. It struck me how similar all the creatures of the world are, sharing the same air, warming themselves with the same sun, drinking and bathing with the same water –every animal, every plant, surviving with the same sources of life. We are all relatives, blood relatives, incestuous relatives, be you plant, animal, Serb, Croat, Jew, Arab, Yankee, Met, –"

"Hey," said Edie, cutting in, "what about the Phillies?"

Sam took a hit of coffee. "OK, the lowly Phillies too."

"Bah – some relative you are."

"And quit cutting in."

"Yes sire, you were saying?"

"I was saying that everything on the planet is related. Our whole concept of family is much too narrow. It should be broadened to include all the living organisms of our world. This provincial, stingy idea of family we cling to so ferociously divides us and artificially turns us into antagonists. If we could broaden our concept of family beyond mom and dad, sister and brother, Uncle Joe, Aunt Ethel and their kids, we might begin to understand that what's good for the whole is good for the individual. I don't think humans understand that." He took a sip of coffee and shook his head. "Woo! Listen to that shit."

They drank their coffee in silence, digesting their food as well as the up country thoughts that had just been set before them. Most people, after the events of the day before, would have fled a gooey examination of the human condition. Most people, after the events of the day before, would do anything to flee reality, to keep the fantasy alive, to keep it light. Most people don't want to think. Most people want to escape. But the heroes of this story were not most people. Their relationship thrived on immersing themselves in such thoughts, not escaping them.

Edie placed her cup on the tray and leaned back on the sofa. "A rather Utopian concept, don't you think?"

Sam continued sipping his morning stimulant. "Sure, it's Utopian, but all advancements in the human condition begin with a Utopian thought."

Edie unconsciously nodded as she continued to ponder the idea. "Why do you only say the 'human condition'? We are talking about the whole family here, aren't we?"

Sam smiled and shook his head. "Edie, sometimes I'm not sure you're supposed to be so smart. Didn't I say something like that last night?"

"Yes – and you know you wouldn't want it any other

way."

He put down his empty cup and, as Edie had done before, leaned back on the sofa. They kissed sweetly on the lips, nibbling on each other, reveling in their newfound status as lovers. "OK, OK," he gathered himself as he began to explain. "Look, all species are doing their darndest to survive. First rule: survive. What I am suggesting is that by being so destructive, by not respecting other life forms, by thinking we are above the concerns of other species, both plant and animal, we are retarding our own evolutionary – what?"

Edie tried to help. "Progress?" Sam seemed unconvinced. "Growth?" He shrugged. "Development?" An arched eyebrow, a skewered expression, nah. "Awareness?"

Ah hah, he reacted immediately. "Yes, awareness. All your other words were in the ballpark but awareness is the trigger for all positive steps into the future. The archaic attitude we have now is even making us less concerned for ourselves. We are still killing each other in assembly line proportions. By broadening our concept of family it would help us rein in our destructive impulses. We would not only be helping the rest of the planet's life forms, but immensely helping ourselves. My attitude is not a 'bleeding heart' attitude. It is firmly anchored in the self interest of my species."

Edie looked at him and smiled. "Beautiful."

Sam decided to play a game they had played earlier in this tale, way back on the other side of lovemaking. "Dear Ann Landers, I don't think humans understand that. What do you think? Signed, Perplexed"

Edie got right into the game. "Dear Perplexed, I think

you'd do better not to think. Better to kiss your wife when you come home from work, to get the NFL package, and to charcoal some steaks on the weekend. Leave the thinking to the public relations people, the CEO's, and the market researchers."

"Not too optimistic, are you?"

She sighed deeply and gazed blankly across the room. The screeching eruption of a brief catfight came through the front door from up the lane. Was it Buster? "Believe me Sam, I feel the same way you do. But Ann Landers and all those of her ilk are tools of the status quo. All I was doing was giving you the acceptable response of the people who fabricate such trash. To be optimistic with regard to the Gillette Gods is a very difficult task. They are so wrapped up in their Stock Markets and economic indicators – they haven't got a clue."

Sam nodded in agreement. "I hear you girl, I hear you. I can remember when I was a little boy and my dad took me to a baseball game at Yankee Stadium. The pitcher was a guy named Early Wynn. Sometime during the game he plunked a guy with a fastball. I said, 'boy, that must hurt.' My dad said Wynn would throw at his own mother if it meant winning a game."

Our fair lady seemed a bit confused. "What do you mean? – that the Gillette Gods would throw at their own mothers if it meant making more money?"

"Or bringing more tourists to South Isle."

"It's true," they accidentally said in chorus, "it's hard to be optimistic."

Chapter 17

Not a Love Story

By now the passionate urges had been placated, the toast and juice had been ingested, the coffee had been drunk, the pets had been fed and a new day had swung into full swing. It seemed to be a perfect time for some kind of parting, but our contented protagonists seemed reluctant to end their initial encounter.

Although, as we know, Sam and Edie had done their fair share of talking since their chance meeting on the Blanco Street Pier, most of it was done in an atmosphere of tension. Each side knew the goal was a successful amorous confluence and everything was tainted by this attempt to consummate this primordial necessity. Lurking beneath each phrase, each topic, each joke or story, was an attempt to conquer the other, to break down barriers, to find common ground, even to conquer oneself. It was hard to enjoy the moment when the stakes were so high.

But now that all the erotic energy had been put to rest, they found themselves basking comfortably in each other's presence. Now that the pressure was off, they wanted to talk even more.

Now they were talking because they wanted to and not because they had to.

Sam continued shaking his head as he thought about the state of the planet. Certainly, there was some consciousness of ecology and stress and other maladies associated with the "New World Order" and the way of life currently being rammed up our asses by the objective news swindlers at Fox and all the rest. But it seemed little more than a prop in the theater of the status quo. Like Jesus so long ago, the Gillette Gods were co-opting these issues for their own purposes.

Edie wondered what Sam was so wrapped up in. She could feel his unrest, as if she'd known him for years. "Sam?" His deeply etched thinking wrinkle appeared between his inquisitive eyes. He hadn't heard her. "Sam!"

Like an exhausted boxer who had just returned to his senses after being sponged off by his trainer, he snapped out of it. "Oh – I'm sorry. You were saying?"

"I could see the wheels were turning." She paused briefly, amused by his retreat into his own mind. "A penny for your thoughts."

"*Humphh*," he grunted, "that would be the going rate for my thoughts these days."

"Well Sam, remember, the best things in life are free. I think we proved that last night." He stared across the room, not knowing what to say. "C'mon boy, tell me what you're thinking, that's what I'm here for."

"You know Edie, you're the greatest." He thought of Ralph and Alice Cramden. He laughed and kissed her on the lips, more lovingly than passionately. "Gosh Edie – geez – I think I'm falling in –"

She quickly put a finger over his lips. "No, no, Sam – I don't want to hear that word. It's been overworked and beaten to death. It's been glamorized, sanitized, homogenized and propagandized. I don't know what it is supposed to mean anymore. This is not a love story. Let's go from here without any blueprints. Let's let it find its own course. I've been pushed down the muck-a-luck love road a few times too many. Whatever I feel for you – I don't want to call it love. I don't want to call it anything."

Sam sat in stunned silence, trying to digest this extraordinary woman's whole persona. Wow! Maybe this had nothing to do with love. Maybe it was time to leave love behind. He was reminded of an old pop tune – "Love Stinks." Was it the J. Giles Band?

She put her arm around his shoulder and kissed him on the cheek. "C'mon, what were you thinking?"

"After all that, you really want to know?"

She shook her head and sighed deeply. "No Sam," she said sarcastically, "I only want to listen because I have ears."

Chapter 18

The Ugliness

"I was thinking," Sam renewed his dissertation, "how hard it was to be optimistic. The Gillette Gods are loose in the open field and there is no one there to stop them – and, as you said, they don't have a clue."

"Unfortunately, their defeated opposition –"

"You mean the Commies and all that?"

"Right." Edie explained. "They didn't seem to have much of a clue either. I remember looking at an atlas one time – I can't remember why, I just love the atlas – and I was looking at a map of Russia. I noticed two islands in the Arctic Ocean that were named October Revolution Island and Bolshevik Revolution Island. I knew right then and there these people were not hip enough to defeat the Gillette Gods."

"I'd have called them the Freeze Your Ass Off Islands." They laughed for a moment and Sam went on. "But at least it represented an idea, something that could be worked on or honed or – who knows? It's true, those people were not nearly ready to take down the Nasdaq cowboys, but they were lashing out at something that needed to be lashed out at."

"You mean like Mike Tyson?"

He paused for a moment, his lips pressed together, his luminous dark eyes glittering in thought. He slowly began to nod affirmatively. "Yes, in a geo-political sense, the Soviet Union was the nation-state version of Mike Tyson."

"And they are not guilty?"

He continued to nod almost imperceptibly as he searched for an answer. "Yes, not guilty. They have erred terribly, they've committed some terribly anti-social acts, but now that they are not around – I mean, look what's happening; the Gillette Gods are bombing whoever they want, whenever they want –" He stopped brusquely and shook his head in disgust. He decided to verbalize something he'd said to himself earlier in this epic. "I'm sorry Edie, good guys and bad guys? No, I don't think so. When it comes to anti-social acts, humanity must shoulder the blame as a unit."

"So we are all guilty?"

"Or not guilty, it's all the same. We are still not ready to get it right and the aggression of the Nasdaq cowboys proves it, and it is not based on anything more than markets and Nike logos. Surely there is something beyond reckless, selfish capitalism and constipated Communism. That can't be the only 2 choices."

Edie placed a finger over her mouth and silently shuffled what she had just heard in her mind. "Interesting," she muttered, as she gathered the coffee tray and walked over to the kitchen. She deposited the dirty cups and utensils in the sink. "I don't suppose such objective philosophical goo would find much favor amongst today's news swindlers."

"I'll clean the dishes," Sam shouted over, "leave them in the sink."

"Oh God, don't worry about it." Edie put the sugar back

in the cupboard and placed the milk in the refrigerator. She then returned to the sofa, folding her legs under her as she looked at our boy.

"Can you remember," she spoke slowly, carefully picking her words, "when you first started feeling – oh – alienated with our culture?"

Sam was reminded of the cab ride home and his thoughts when they were sitting behind the garbage truck. "Do you remember the ride home last night?"

"Sam," she replied quietly, "I'll never forget that ride home."

"Me neither." He smiled and went on. "Anyway, you can't believe some of the things I was thinking in that cab."

"Me too. I got to thinking about the price of gasoline."

He looked at her in a confused way. "The price of gasoline?"

"It's a long story." She shrugged. "What about you?"

"Do you remember when we were behind the big garbage truck?"

She scrunched her face in thought. "Garbage truck?"

"You don't remember the garbage truck?"

She thought some more. "Sorry."

"Oh well, believe me, there was a garbage truck and it triggered some long gone memories."

He explained the whole story with Moby Garbage Truck and the American flag on its rear and how it helped him to decide to leave the city –and all that. When he was done, they sat for awhile in silence. Edie began thinking about her own Rubicon crossings.

"I think there was a similar moment for me," she said cautiously, trying to focus in on her memory, "but it was probably just the culmination of a slow trip to the brink."

Sam nodded in agreement. "Yes, it would have to be. We are talking about the proverbial straw that broke the camel's back, aren't we?"

"I think," Edie went on without acknowledging Sam's remark, "long before I had it explained to myself; long before I was conscious of the rat race, or ecology, or whatever specific madness we can associate with the Gillette Gods and their way of life –" she paused, trying to get it right "– I think it was the ugliness that planted the seed of my discontent. Somehow, the suburban sprawl, the plastic signs, the whole landscape of the American Dream began to – I don't know. You get it, don't you?"

"Sure. What do you think I was looking at that day behind Moby?"

Edie looked around her simple but elegant living room. She wondered if she was being hypocritical with her cutesy knick-knack business. Wasn't she getting sucked in? Wasn't she becoming one of them? No, she thought, what she did was different. This wasn't some impersonal hustle built upon some elaborate market analysis. Nobody was being "targeted" here, nobody was being scientifically persuaded to buy, to want, to need. A little piece of herself went into every one of her designs.

Now it was Sam's turn to delve into Edie's mind. "Two cents for your thoughts."

"Wow, 2 cents! What do we have here, inflation?"

"Whatever that is."

She continued to stare blankly across the room, thinking back more than 20 years. "I think there was a moment –" She tried to collect her thoughts.

"What was it?" Sam tried to help, "a moment of recognition, like my day with the garbage truck?"

"Well – when I was back in the world of political science, my older brother lived close to campus. He'd been married about 4 years and had two beautiful little kids, a girl and a boy. He'd bought a nice house in the 'burbs and was doing pretty well."

"What does he do?"

"An accountant."

"A likely story."

She half smirked and half laughed. "Anyway, I was at an age when serious mate seeking was part of the plan. My brother and his life was the natural path for me to follow and for awhile I bought it – or maybe I could see no other viable lifestyle. Someday I would marry someone just like him and I'd be the wife his wife was, etc., etc."

"A likely story."

"I suppose most of us are sprung from likely stories." Once again, she put her finger to her mouth and continued shuffling around in her memory. "As time went on – well – I started to feel uncomfortable in that house. I had very little to say to my sister-in-law, in fact, my brother seemed to have very little to say to my sister-in-law. She picked the tile for the bathroom, he watched the Phillies on TV; she went to Lord & Taylor's, he went golfing; she spent the money, he read the Wall Street Journal. In the future the little girl would go to ballet class and the little boy would be in the Little League. Now that the 2 or 3 years of passionate secretions were becoming fewer and further between, the only thing that really brought them together was when the older child surreptitiously did something to make the younger one cry. This meant my brother would have to put down the paper, or stop watching the game, and lay down the law."

"Daddy," said Sam, with a stern voice, "gets tough."

Edie was not in a humorous mood. She shook her head and stared down at the coffee table. She spoke to the coffee table. "After awhile, I began to think, Jesus, this is what I'm shooting for? This is what I want?" She turned and looked at Sam once again. "It was after one of those visits to my brother's house that I quit school. A few weeks later I had a little money saved and I hit the road. It wasn't much longer before my fate deposited me here at the end of the road, like a turd falling into a toilet, along with the rest of the cultural refuse that once made this place so special."

That longing for the "old days" in South Isle, like a dose of heartburn that always seemed to come back, came over Sam. "Until people like your brother and his wife," he said sadly, "began making money for Tom Lento."

Edie got up first. She held her hand out. Sam grabbed it. She helped pull him to his feet. They embraced warmly. They parted and looked at each other. Sam could not help but ask, almost in a whisper, "When will we see each other again?"

She shrugged and smiled timidly. "It shouldn't take long."

"It's a date then." He kissed her and looked into her eyes. "I don't love you."

"I don't love you either." They kissed again and Sam headed for the door.

Chapter 19

The End

When a cold front sweeps across South Isle, the old wooden homes that are so emblematic of the place have a peculiar characteristic: they seem to hold the cold air a bit longer than the duration of the cold weather.

When Sam stepped through the front door and out into the lane, he immediately felt the difference. A light but steady breeze was coming from the southeast and the humidity – a not uncomfortable humidity – hit him in the face like a moist towel. He was now overdressed in his long sleeved Marlins jersey with the ketchup stain on the collar. He wished he were in a pair of shorts.

But the pleasant winter warmth felt great. He stretched his arms way up over his head and took the full brunt of the sun on his medieval moneychanger's face. When he started up the lane, he noticed all the colors of the abundant vegetation – the bougainvilleas, the hibiscus, the thumburgia, the coral vine, the varying shades of green embodied in the trees and vines invading the lane, even the quality of the darkened shade – seemed more vivid and alive in the late morning sun. When he got to the top of the lane, he remembered he'd forgotten the jacket he'd loaned Edie the night before.

He stopped and began to turn around. He stopped again. He smiled slyly and continued on his way.

A rooster with a bad timepiece crowed strongly in the distance.

About the Author

Jerome Grapel was born in Brooklyn, NY in 1945 and raised in the New York City area in what could be called a vintage middle class upbringing. He attended Temple University in Philadelphia where He played baseball and graduated with a B.A. in history in 1967. With a noticeable lack of vocation for anything, and not knowing what else to do, he continued at Temple Law School, graduating in 1970.

After a short stint at a small law firm, Grapel's courtship with the American Dream ended unsuccessfully. In 1972, a friend from college introduced him to Key West, the perfect antidote for cultural misfits. He has lived there ever since, working a multitude of inconsequential jobs, none of which had to be taken home with him. For the last 30 years he has been driving a taxi, a job which offered the flexibility to travel extensively. Without a "career" to encumber much of his life, he began writing in his spare time. "I found out this is what I want to do," he says.

Grapel has been married 2 times but has grown accustomed to living alone over the last 20 years or so. It is also relevant to note that for much of that time he has spent two months of the year on the Spanish island of Formentera. *Not A Love Story* is his first work of fiction.

AbsolutelyAmazingEbooks.com

or AA-eBooks.com

www.ingramcontent.com/pod-product-compliance
Lightning Source LLC
Chambersburg PA
CBHW070443030726
47503CB00004B/866